William Dowling

The names and titles of our Lord and Savior Jesus Christ as given in the New Testament

William Dowling

The names and titles of our Lord and Savior Jesus Christ as given in the New Testament

ISBN/EAN: 9783741189968

Manufactured in Europe, USA, Canada, Australia, Japa

Cover: Foto ©Andreas Hilbeck / pixelio.de

Manufactured and distributed by brebook publishing software (www.brebook.com)

William Dowling

The names and titles of our Lord and Savior Jesus Christ as given in the New Testament

PREFACE.

THE Names and Titles of our ever-blessed Lord and Saviour are concentrated and beautiful descriptions of His most glorious work. They declare what He has been, what He is, and what He ever will be to His Church. Each speaks volumes of heavenly truth to spiritual hearts. Some of these comprehensive names guide us to His hallowing cross, others attract us to the brightness of His throne.

By contemplating these sacred and suggestive titles, believers in Jesus may hope to increase their faith, purify their love, and learn more of the Great Master's holy will.

Controversy has been excluded from the following meditations, the object being to

promote evangelical religion in Christians of
every communion.

The Names and Titles have been selected
from the New Testament only, that the work
might be kept within a small compass. The
various titles have been arranged in twelve
groups, a classification which collects around a
few defined centres the ideas revealed in many
detached passages. Each group has its own
distinctive heading, and is followed by a short
paragraph suggesting the ideas which connect
the respective titles in each of the twelve
classes.

May the Holy Spirit shed upon each reader
those rays of heavenly light which reveal to
believing hearts the reality and glory of our
Lord's mediatorial work !

CONTENTS.

———

THE

NAMES AND TITLES

OF

Our Lord and Saviour Jesus Christ.

SECTION I.

Titles of our Lord

AS

THE ANOINTED, INCARNATE, AND DIVINE SAVIOUR.

JESUS.
THE CHRIST.
EMMANUEL.

THESE three titles bring before us the great "mystery of godliness." *Jesus*, the Divine Redeemer, accomplishing man's salvation by sufferings too awful to be comprehended : *Christ*, the appointed Saviour, chosen for the glorious work before the creation of the world : and *Emmanuel*, uniting, in one mysterious nature, suffering humanity with the infinite Godhead.   B

JESUS.

This name is the Greek form of the Hebrew word Joshua, a contraction of Jehoshua, signifying "the help of Jehovah"; or, "the Lord the Saviour." The reader will, doubtless, remember that the original name of Joshua was Oshea,* a word denoting *help*, which Moses changed to Jehoshua, when appointing the future captain of Israel one of the twelve explorers of the land of Canaan. The Apostle regarded Joshua as a type of our Saviour;† and a well-informed faith can trace many resemblances between him who led the Israelites into Egypt after their long wanderings, and the Great Captain of our salvation, who will assuredly lead the whole army of believers into the rest that remaineth "to the people of God."‡ As the name Jesus has the same signification as Jehoshua, we see that it signifies not simply "Saviour," but a *Saviour appointed by Jehovah*. This view will lead all Christian hearts to feel a peculiar and solemn force in the words of the angel, "Thou shalt call His name Jesus."§ He who descended from heaven to rescue men, might well be called "Jehovah's Saviour," the most precious gift of the Father to a fallen world.

The name of Jesus is "above every name." The

---

* Numb. xiii. 16.
† Heb. iv. 8. The reader will see that "Jesus" here is only the Greek name of Joshua.
‡ Heb. iv. 9.   § Matt. i. 21.

reason is evident when we turn to the Cross. There was finished a work above every work. There a complete salvation was prepared. There the grand freedom was proclaimed.

This name contains a meaning too vast to be fully comprehended by us. It directs our wandering gaze to the heights of glory, and also leads us to sit in adoring silence at the Cross.

It reminds us of that complete deliverance from sin which the Saviour has promised to all His redeemed. A period is really coming when, in the future state, *perfection* shall be theirs.* Let us dwell, for a moment, on this thought. Then we shall never think wrongly, never feel wrongly. Always be willing to do just what the Lord wills. Be as conscious of His presence as of our own existence. Ever be delighting in that presence. Becoming so purified as "to see God."† Always living in the light of heaven, and receiving, through eternity, the hallowing rays of the " Sun of Righteousness." We shall live with the bright host of the saved, all blessed for ever in Him. Not one discord, moral or mental, will break the glorious harmony.

But must we wait for this salvation until the life that now is be over? No; for Jesus is a *present* Saviour. The beginnings of this heavenly life must be felt here. The trees which are to flourish in Paradise are first planted in Christ's vineyard on earth. The question is not, Are we *now* perfect?

* Heb. xii. 23.   † Mat. v. 8.

but, Are we pressing "toward the mark"?* Are we "looking unto Jesus"?†

This name reminds us of a deliverer from condemnation. "I am guilty" is the first utterance of a divinely-awakened soul. Turning to the Cross, the true penitent reads the words of mercy, "He is the propitiation for our sins."‡ What then remains to be done? Happy they who receive the free gospel in all its fulness. But mistakes are often made. One thinks it presumptuous to expect so rich a gift as a full pardon,"without money and without price."§ Here the freeness of the Father's mercy in Christ is doubted. The sufficiency of the great sacrifice is denied. The merit of a sinner's work is asserted. In truth, the whole Gospel is contradicted. Another deceives himself with a false humility. "I am not worthy yet to receive salvation," is the delusive confession. So he waits until he may have more repentance, more faith, more of self, which he may offer to God as a sacrifice. Such sinners want to be their own Saviours.

But the truly regenerate man comes just as he is to the Cross. Has he been the most wicked man upon the earth, he comes to the perfect sacrifice. Has he been an apostate and denied the Lord? A terrible case; but he comes to receive the infinite atonement. Thus the believer in Jesus glories in the Lord alone. Such only understand the full meaning of the holy name Jesus

* Philip. iii. 14.   † Heb. xii. 2.   ‡ 1 John ii. 2.   § Isa. lv. 1.

The souls of the redeemed in heaven and Christians struggling with sin on earth, are *now* one family by the power of this name.* We sometimes visit, with sorrowing but hopeful hearts, the silent resting places of loved ones formerly with us. What links them to us still ? The name of Jesus. They *sleep* in Him,† and we *live* in Him.‡

The history of this sacred word reminds us of its uniting power. Derived from the Hebrew, adopted by the Greek, received into the Latin, and carried over the earth in hundreds of languages, it is now binding together many nations.

Is not this a strengthening name ? " All things are possible to him that believeth,"§ are the remarkable words of the Lord. By faith in Him, the heart that was yesterday like a " bruised reed," may to-day be like a "cedar of Lebanon." "Learn to live," says one moralist; "learn to die," is the teaching of another. Great lessons both, but who is sufficient for these things?‖ What is the assuring answer of Jesus ? " My grace is sufficient for thee."¶ On this let us rest, and say with a bold humility, we " can do all things through Christ."**

The Christ.

The Messiah—The *Christ*—The *Anointed* One—are names which have kindled glorious hopes in every age. Our Lord was anointed for His great work,

* Eph. iii. 15. † 1 Thess. iv. 14. ‡ Phil. i. 21. . § Mark ix. 23.
‖ 2 Cor. ii. 16. ¶ 2 Cor. xii. 9. ** Philip. iv. 13.

even " before the foundation of the world."* The
holy angels may therefore have pondered over this
mystery long before the human family was created.
Man sinned, and immediately The Christ was foretold.† But to whom was this first prediction in the
Bible uttered ? To the wicked spirit. Thus satanic
pride was checked, while a bright ray of heavenly
hope fell upon the earth.

This ancient prophecy is a summary of man's
history, and of his redemption. It tells of the long
and mysterious war between light and darkness. It
also tells of a glorious victory. " The head " of
Satan shall be bruised. By whom ? By the seed of
the woman. Thus the Bible begins as it ends, with
ascribing salvation to the Lord alone.

How long the Church sometimes waits for the
accomplishment of her Lord's promises ! The patriarchs looked for the coming Christ. Abraham saw
the distant day.‡ Jacob spake of the expected
Shiloh.§ Moses foretold the Great Prophet.|| David
beheld from afar the sufferings and triumphs of the
Messiah.¶ Isaiah sounded the note of preparation.**

----

* 1 Peter i. 20.

† Gen. iii. 15. The ancient traditions of mankind generally regard
the serpent as the symbol of evil. The Persian wicked spirit, Ahriman,
was said to have led men to sin by tempting them in the form of a
serpent. The Greek deity Apollo is represented as destroying the
great serpent Python. One of the sculptured Hindoo divinities is
trampling on the head of a serpent. Such are the echoes of Gen. iii. 15.

‡ John viii. 56.   § Gen. xlix. 10. || Deut. xviii. 15.

¶ Ps. cx. ii.; xvi. 10 ; xxii. 18 ; xl. 6, 7.

** Isa. xl. 3.

The last of the prophets predicted a sudden coming.* Amidst all this expectation long ages passed away. The kingdom of David was rent, the temple ruined, and Judah sat as an exile by the waters of Babylon, yet the Messiah came not. The long delay, doubtless, often perplexed the Jewish heart with an agony of doubt. Learn to wait, was the great lesson taught to Israel then, as to the Christian now.

But the long night passed away. What did the morning shew? "The Desire of all nations"† had come. On the banks of the Jordan men saw him *anointed* with the Holy Ghost. Did the earth celebrate a grand jubilee? How mysterious, how awful, was the rejection of The Christ! He came in the city predicted,‡ of the tribe and family designated,§ and at the exact time foretold.‖ Yet was he "despised and rejected."¶ Twenty-four false Messiahs have, at various times, won favour with the Jews, in whose ancient metropolis the true Messiah was crucified. Eighteen centuries have passed away, and He is yet to the Jews "a stumbling block."** This shall surely be counted among the marvels of human history.††

But a time is coming when even the Jews shall hail as "blessed" the long-rejected Messiah. When shall these things be? How shall they be accomplished? The wise-hearted will be slow to answer.

* Mal. iii. 1.   † Hag. ii. 7.   ‡ Mic. v. 2.   § Isa. xi. 1.
‖ Dan. ix. 25.   ¶ Isa. liii. 3.   ** 1 Cor. i. 23.
†† Some Jewish Rabbins have endeavoured to escape from their difficulties by imagining two Messiahs: one, doomed to suffering, the son of Joseph; the other triumphant, the son of David.

They will rather wait, in faith and prayer, the Father's good pleasure. The routine of the world will most assuredly be broken up by a grand personal manifestation of Christ. That will be the crowning wonder of earth's history.

The High Priests received the title "Anointed," from the rite by which they were appointed.* So important was this ceremony deemed, that special directions were given for preparing the "holy ointment" from the four spices, pure myrrh, sweet cinnamon, sweet calamus, and cassia, added to olive oil; the very proportions being also carefully specified.† The religious Jew would see a deep significance in such special and minute provisions. The superstitious Rabbins of later ages maintained that the consecrating ointment, first made for the anointing of Aaron, never needed replenishing, but lasted for about nine hundred years, down to the time of the captivity. The tradition shews the importance attached by the Jew to the anointing. He, therefore, by the title Messiah, or its Greek equivalent, Christ, ought to have been reminded of that everlasting Priest who was to come in the place of all typical priesthoods. Men may even now, in heart, reject The Christ, by neglecting His priestly sacrifice and intercession, and thus refusing Him as the only anointed of the Father.

* In such passages as Lev. iv. 3, 5, the words "that is anointed," are simply translations of the Hebrew word *Messiah*.

† See Ex. xxx. 23, 24. Taking the shekel at half-an-ounce, there would be 250 ounces each of myrrh and cassia, and 125 ounces each of the other spices.

. The title Christ sets the Lord before us as the Great Prophet, for to this office men were appointed under the old dispensation by anointing.* Moses excited the expectations of Israel by predicting the coming of a Prophet like unto himself, their law-giver and leader.† When the Anointed One appeared in due time, the mighty works done by Him com-pelled the awe-stricken multitude to exclaim, " a great prophet is risen up among us."‡ Christ, long before his appearance on earth, spoke by the spirit of prophecy, which is called "The Spirit of Christ."§ As a prophet he unfolded the coming. desolation of Jerusalem, and to the insulting Jewish Council pre-dicted His own " coming in the clouds of heaven."‖ The mocking officers directed their ignorant sarcasms against the prophetical office of the Saviour in the words, " Prophesy unto us, thou Christ, Who is he that smote thee ?"¶

The " Christ," or the Anointed One, also reminds us of that *kingly* office under which the multitude gladly received Him, under which ancient seers beheld Him,** which He bore on the cross, and now claims in heaven. David was three times anointed,†† each time by his fellow men, but Christ, the " King of kings," received one anointing for ever from the everlasting Father.‡‡ It was as the anointed King, as " Messiah the Prince,"§§ He was revealed unto

---

* 1 Kings, xix. 16. ‖ Matt. xxvi. 64. ‡‡ Matt. iii. 16.
† Deut. xviii. 15, 18. ¶ Matt. xxvi. 68. §§ Dan. ix. 25.
‡ Luke vii. 16. ** Zech. ix. 9.
§ 1 Peter i. 11. †† 1 Sam. xvi. 1, 13 ; 2 Sam. ii. 4 ; v. 3.

Daniel, while engaged in his evening supplications; and as a king over the whole heart, the Lord is received by every worshipping disciple. We depend for salvation on The " Christ," for as the anointed Priest He is our "propitiation"; we look to "Christ" for wisdom, for as the anointed Prophet He speaks now by His Word and by His Spirit; we worship "Christ," for as the anointed King His statutes are the guides of our life.

Thus honouring Christ as Priest, Prophet, and King, the Christian receives from God the Father a holy anointing, and that hallowing "unction" which, abiding on the soul,* elevates even weak followers of Christ to become priests and kings unto God. Thus Christ, the Anointed One, makes Christians to be His anointed ones, and so like to Himself.

EMMANUEL.

Matt. i. 23. (And see Isa. vii. 14; viii. 8.)

THREE times only is this word used in the Bible; twice in the Old Testament, and once in the New. Our Lord was never addressed by the name Emmanuel, but that He was " God with us," both His works and words declared. " He that hath seen Me, hath seen the Father,"† was the answer of Jesus to Philip, praying, " Lord, shew us the Father." The " fulness of the Godhead "‡ was there close to Philp, though the weak disciple knew

* 1 John ii. 20   † John xiv. 9.   ‡ Col. ii. 9.

it not. Are not many of Christ's followers often in a similar state of unconsciousness? The Lord is walking with them, in evident providences, in solemn influences, but their eyes are "holden."[*] What a surpassingly grand event does this name Emmanuel suggest! "God with us," once walking in a human form to and fro upon the earth; seen and heard by tens of thousands; at one time proclaiming life-giving truths in populous cities; at another listening to the prejudices, the misrepresentations, the passionate invectives, and even the sarcasms of His own fallen creatures.[†] The marvellous history is written in words bright as sun-light, and proved by miracles wrought in the open day, before multitudes, in the presence of bitter and powerful foes. When the great roll of this world's history shall be full, many "things too wonderful"[‡] for understanding will be there, but most amazing will be the fact that, "God was manifest in the flesh."[§]

How wonderfully near to the Eternal Godhead has this brought man! He was created "a little lower than the angels;"[||] but in Emmanuel human nature is crowned with glory and honour. The Lord of Glory has trodden the highway of human life. He knows, by His own experience, all its rough places and dangerous turns. In what part of the road are we now? He has been there before

---

* Luke xxiv. 16. † Luke vii. 34; John x. 20, 33. ‡ Job xlii. 3.
§ 1 Tim. iii. 16. || Heb. ii. 7.

us.   He is even now guiding the storm-beaten ship
of His Church over the swelling waters.   Many
disciples,—the watching and praying ones,—can
hear, amid the tempest, His quieting words, "It is
I; be not afraid."

Ages before the Lord was manifested in the flesh,
He was pleased to make Himself known to His
ancient people, under various most expressive
forms.   Abraham beheld Him on the plains of
Mamre, and acknowledged His power by that
impressive intercessory prayer for the guilty city,
which is a model to us of earnest, persevering
supplication.*   In human form the Son shewed
Himself to Jacob by the lonely ford of the Jabbok,†
where the amazed and blessed patriarch felt that he
had "seen God face to face."‡

About two centuries-and-a-half passed away, and
then was manifested another marvellous appearance,
not this time in a human shape, but as a mysterious
fire—bright, yet not comsuming.   Thus to Moses,
in the solitudes of Horeb, did Emmanuel reveal
Himself in a visible form and by that most glorious
name which the Saviour claimed as His own before
the prejudiced and angry Jews.§   The guiding
cloud, the pillar of fire, and the awful manifestations
at the giving of the law on Sinai, were revelations
of Christ, as Emmanuel, to "the Church in the

* Gen. xviii.   † This name probably implies "wrestling."
‡ Gen. xxxii. 30; and Hos. xii. 4, 5.   The name "Peniel," given by
    Jacob to the place, signifies, "the face of God."
    § Ex. iii. 4, 6, 14; and John viii. 58.

wilderness."* When Moses heard the mysterious "voice of one speaking to him from off the mercy-seat,"† he listened to the words of the Son, who was with the people in the "tabernacle of witness." The Jews had not heard the Father's "voice at any time:"‡ these revelations from the mercy-seat were, therefore, the words of the ever-blessed Son, who thus, in early ages, was present as God with men. All these preparatory manifestations ended, in "the fulness of time," by the incarnation of the Divine Word, by His voluntary humiliation among His own creatures, His great teachings, and His propitiatory sacrifice.

Even now, though the visible presence of Christ be, for a time, withdrawn, we must regard Him as "God with us." "I am with you alway,"§ were the parting words by which the Saviour strengthened the hearts of the first disciples, and their truth is being daily verified still.

A few more ages may be allowed to the present dispensation, and "then cometh the end,"‖ when the whole Church, united in one family, shall behold Emmanuel, and hear the heavenly announcement— "The Tabernacle of God is with men!"¶

There can, therefore, be no final defeat for the Church of Christ. In the great warfare of souls the victory is sure. Let us then learn to mark His goings forth upon the earth. The daily history of the world, all the signs of the times, are but the

* Acts vii. 38.   † Num. vii. 89.   ‡ John v. 37.
§ Matt xxviii. 20.   ‖ 1 Cor. xv. 24.   ¶ Rev. xxi. 3.

unfolding of His purposes. News from the East and from the West, rumours from the North and from the South, do but whisper in the ear of Faith that our Emmanuel is working out the eternal decrees. The nations may be perplexed, and the earth be shaking, but let the Church of Christ be still, "and see the salvation of the Lord."* The tumult shall ere long be hushed, and there shall be a great calm in that new Jerusalem, where the redeemed shall walk in everlasting light, "and God Himself shall be with them!"†

* Ex. xiv. 13.   † Rev. xxi. 3.

Titles of our Lord

IN

HIS HUMAN NATURE.

THE SON OF DAVID.
THE NAZARENE.
THE ROOT OF DAVID.
THE LION OF THE TRIBE OF JUDAH.
THE SON OF MAN.

THESE five titles declare the Lord's humanity. As *the Son of David*, we see in Him the long predicted descendant of the great king and prophet of Israel. *The Nazarene* bids us remember the lowliness of His human condition: as *the Root of David*, we behold Him in close and mysterious alliance with one special family of Abraham's line: as the *Lion of the Tribe of Judah*, we behold a glorious power and grand pre-eminence belonging to the "Man of Sorrows:" and as *The Son of Man*, we see Him treading all the paths of human suffering.

THE SON OF DAVID.

Matt i. 1; ix. 27; xv. 22; xx. 30; xxi. 9; xxii. 42.

The house of David is no longer ranked with the royal families of the earth. But the Lord of Glory, being in His human nature David's son, has conferred an imperishable honour on the name of the sweet singer of Israel. The mightiest of the ancient dynasties, the most famous of modern kingly lines, have no renown compared with this!

This title of our Lord seems to have been especially popular. The blind men, in their intense anxiety for relief, call Him by that name.[*] The sorrowing woman of Canaan expressed her reverence by this title.[†] The applauding multitude filled Jerusalem with the shout, "Hosanna to the Son of David!"[‡] The Pharisees agreed in this feeling with the common people.[§] It was, indeed, a matter for national exultation, that the great Restorer of all things was the Son of their ancient and favourite king. The thought might well console the Jew who mourned under the iron yoke of heathen Rome.

But for our Lord Himself this title secured little honour, if we except the short-lived applause of the fickle crowd. The Son of David had no settled home, even of the meanest kind.[||] He was despised by the thoughtless people for the lowliness of His

---

[*] Matt. ix. 27; xx. 30.   [†] Matt. xv. 22.   [‡] Matt. xxi. 9.
[§] Matt. xxii. 42.   [||] Matt. viii. 20.

social rank,* and was sometimes wearied and thirsty in the mid-day heat of a Syrian sun.†

What a startling contrast was then seen upon the earth! The proud, cruel, and wicked Emperor Tiberius, had the treasures and pomp of the Roman world at his feet. The pure, loving, and divine Son of David was exposed to want, insult, and shame!

Through the far distance of a thousand years, David had beheld, in prophetic vision, the sufferings and exaltation of this Son. He foresaw every solemn accompaniment of the crucifixion. The nails, the mocking, the lots cast for the garments, and the gaze of the heartless crowd.‡ To David was also given the view of his glorious Son's exaltation.§ Without this, the awful gloom of Calvary might have been too dark a prospect even for a prophet's eye.

The name of David, signifying, *Beloved*, was especially appropriate to him, as a type of the "beloved Son," who is set forth as the most decisive proof of the love of God toward man. The law of love is the great ruling principle of the Redeemer's kingdom, so important in its effects, that the Lord calls it a "new commandment."‖

David defeated the giant, one of the mightiest enemies of Israel, and thus was a figure of the great Conqueror who first broke the might of Satan, and will, ere long, imprison the deceiving host in the bottomless pit.

* Matt. xiii. 55.   † John iv. 6.   ‡ Ps. xxii. 8, 16, 18.
§ Ps. cx.; and xlv. 6.   ‖ John xiii. 34.

The Son of Jesse bore the three characters of
Prophet, Priest, and King;* being, therefore, a
full and significant type of the Saviour in these
His great offices.

David enlarged his dominions by a long series of
conquests, and gained "a great name,"† being in
these particulars, also, a representative of the victorious Redeemer, who must ultimately rule over
"the kingdoms of this world,"‡ and at whose
name the universe shall bow.§ "Thy throne shall
be established for ever,"‖ was the promise made
to David; and as the throne of the glorified Son of
David is, "for ever and ever,"¶ the prediction
will be completely accomplished. The Jew may,
in vain, be expecting the restoration of his nation's
ancient glory, but the Christian sees the throne of
David made perpetual in the person and rule of the
everlasting Son.

How great is the mystery of the Incarnation!
No marvel that some reject the amazing doctrine!
The mere human reason is utterly confounded in
the presence of so sublime a fact! That the Lord
of Eternal Glory should become the Son of one of
His own creatures, may well engage the reverent
meditations of the angels!** Let us fall low in
adoring love before the "Son of David," dedicating
ourselves to Him who thus mysteriously took our
nature upon Him.

---

* 2 Sam. vi. 17; 1 Chron. xvi. 2; Acts ii. 30.   † 2 Sam. vii. 9.
‡ Rev. xi. 15;   § Phil. ii. 10.   ‖ 2 Sam. vii. 16.   ¶ Heb. i. 8.
** 1 Pet. i. 12.

The Nazarene.

Matt. ii. 23.

There is but one town on the earth which gave a name to the Lord of Glory. Rome, Athens, even Jerusalem were passed over, and the honour fell on a small, rustic, and despised town of Galilee. The prophet had foretold, more than seven centuries before, that Messiah would be "despised;"[*] and thus it followed that His name became associated with a place held in contempt even by the Jews. " Can there any good thing come out of Nazareth ?"[†] was the natural question of the honest-hearted Nathaniel. It seems strange that illiterate Nazareth should have been selected for the abode of Him in whom were " all the treasures of wisdom and knowledge."[‡] Christ was foretold by Isaiah,[§] as " a branch " from Jesse; and the same prophet represents the Messiah as " a root (sprout or branch) out of a dry ground;"[||]—the ideas thus suggested are those of royalty, and yet of contempt. The Hebrew word, " Nētsĕr," translated, " a sprout," or " a branch," is thought to have been the ancient name of Nazareth. Three prophets, Isaiah, Jeremiah,[¶] and Zechariah,[**] foretold the Saviour by this name. St. Matthew therefore was led to use the plural, "prophets," when referring to these

---

[*] Isa. liii. 3.   [†] John i. 46.   [‡] Col. ii. 3.   [§] Isa. xi. 1.   [||] Isa. liii. 2.   [¶] Jer. xxiii. 5; xxxiii. 15.   [**] Zech. iii. 8; vi. 12.

ancient predictions. "He shall be called a Nazarene," seems to combine the idea of lowliness
with that of contempt, associated with the despised
city of Nazareth.

Here is another impressive proof that God's ways
are not as our ways. Man would surely have
selected a home for so sublime a Teacher in some
great centre of learning and intellect! He who
doeth all things well, chose Nazareth.

In that lowly city, seated in its beautiful and quiet
vale, begirt by the hills of Galilee, and with Mount
Tabor full in view, the glorious Saviour passed in a
mysterious silence about thirty years of His marvellous life. In one of its houses the Lord of all
worked as a carpenter; in its street He walked;
with its people He conversed; in its synagogue
He read the prophecy of His grand mission; and
there the infuriated people assailed Him with
murderous intent. No wonder then that His name
was linked with Nazareth, that He was "called a
Nazarene!"

The devils knew Him as "Jesus of Nazareth,"*
—the common people thus spoke of Him,†—the
angels knew the name,‡—the disciples so described
their Master,§—the enemies of Christ used the title,||
—Jesus Himself acknowledged it, both on earth and
in heaven,¶—the Cross bore it on high,**—and
miracles were wrought by it.††

* Mark i. 24.   † Mark xiv. 67.   ‡ Mark xvi. 6.   § Acts ii. 22.
|| John xviii. 5.   ¶ Ib; and Acts xxii. 8.   ** John xix. 19.
†† Acts iii. 6.

Not only was the Lord "called a Nazarene," but His followers also; the "sect of the Nazarenes" being the contemptuous description applied by their foes.*

In all this we see the humility of our Saviour, and how He made Himself of "no reputation." A stoop from heaven to an earthly throne would have been surprising!—a stoop from heaven to Nazareth confounds us!

If thus the Lord of all willingly descended for us, how low are we willing to be abased for Him and for His Gospel! Do we ever turn aside from His work, lest we should lose some title of honour, or incur some term of contempt? Even here, in a Christian land, the words of scorn are often prepared for those who are resolved to do the great Master's work. He was willing, for us, to be "called· a Nazarene;" if, then, the Master bore contempt, shall the servants dare to shrink? Shall we be ashamed or reluctant to distribute religious books, to visit the sick, to seek out the lost in their dens of misery, or to speak for the honour of Christ?

THE ROOT OF DAVID.

Rev. v. 5; xxii. 16.

The word translated root, in these and many other passages, may also denote that which springs from the root, and therefore will often signify a stem or a

---

* Acts xxiv. 5; and so in some Eastern countries to this day.

branch. This latter image is alone proper to express
the connection of Christ's human nature with the
family of David. The Messiah was repeatedly thus
represented to the Old Testament Church. Isaiah
described the hope of Israel, as "a rod out of the
stem of Jesse, and a Branch shall grow out of his
roots."* In another passage, the "root (branch) of
Jesse"† becomes "an ensign" of the people. The
image of an "ensign" is in harmony with that of a
stem on a hill top, but not at all in accordance with
the notion of a "root," which could not stand for an
ensign. The prophet Jeremiah depicts the coming
Saviour as a righteous "branch" of David;‡ and
Zechariah uses one emphatic noun only—"The
Branch,"§ when exciting the expectations of the
long exiled Jews, and leading them to look for
greater marvels than those witnessed by their fore-
fathers. St. Paul adapts the image used by Isaiah.||
Thus the Saviour was regarded as the branch
springing from the ancient stem of Jesse by
prophets, apostles, and the heavenly host.¶ Our
Lord applies this title to Himself in the last words
of inspiration spoken to St. John.**

"The branch from the stem" of David affords
another illustration of that close union which Christ
has been pleased to establish between man and His
own glorious nature. As the branch partakes of
the qualities of the stem, and as the Lord sprang,
according to His humanity, from the house and

* Isa. xi. 1.   † Isa. xi. 10.   ‡ Jeremiah xxxiii. 15.   § Zech. iii. 8.
|| Rom. xv. 12.   ¶ Rev. v. 5.   ** Rev. xxii. 16.

lineage of. David, it follows that He has taken upon
Himself the whole nature of man, putting only its
sin aside. What a lesson is taught here! The
beggar and the king, a Cæsar and his serf, are alike
branches of one stock; and from that stock He
came, who is "King of kings." If He thus honoured
fallen humanity, shall we dare to despise one of its
weakest, broken, or half-withered branches? Dare
we launch, with keen delight, our sarcastic darts,
and direct our irony against the feeblest of mankind? Shall we mock at human infirmities, or even
at the follies of earth's poor, crippled and blind
children? Pause awhile, keen satirist; check the
stinging irony; for the intended victims are the
brethren of Jesus Christ! Let them be mean,
silly, ignorant, and wicked, they are those whose
nature the Lord of Glory took, and for whom the
Lamb of God was made an everlasting sacrifice.
Will you wound the hearts whom Jesus came to
heal? or deride those over whom the Great Teacher
wept? Let the thought that Christ has condescended to be "a branch" of a human family, and
therefore a kinsman of all, lead us to treat men
reverently, pitying even where we condemn, and
lifting up the fallen, instead of crushing them into
deeper ruin, by wicked arrogance or Pharisean
pride! Thus learning to "honour all men" from
Christian principle, and not according to the rules
of social *etiquette*, we shall, though in a low degree,
imitate Him who descended from the everlasting
mansions, to become a "root" or branch of the
house of David.

Some roots have produced deadly trees; some
branches have been laden with glittering but fatal
fruits. These have long flourished on the earth,
and many nations still love to dwell beneath the
baleful shade. The deadly qualities of the Java
upas tree is mainly the creation of human fancy
and exaggeration; but the moral upas trees of the
world are terrible realities. Over what multitudes
do the branches of Heathen ignorance, Mahommedan
delusion, and Popish superstition extend even now !
They will one day be rooted up, with all plants not
of the Father's planting;* in the meantime, their
shadows darken many nations. But the earth has
one living "Branch," laden with the fruits of
heaven, the very leaves of which provide medicine†
for sin-stricken multitudes. This far-extending
"Branch" of the Tree of Life is now a shelter
for wearied souls, who hasten from the burning
and parched deserts of earth.

The wild fables of the North‡ speak of the Tree
of Life, which sheds its influence over creation, and
hides beneath its roots the fountain of wisdom.
What the rude, untutored heart of the Pagan
imagined, that Christ is in reality. He is the
"Branch" whence living fruit is alone procured,
and He provides the fountain which is ever "springing up into everlasting life."§ Whatever good the
poetic fancies of the ancient poets have depicted
in the visions of their long past golden age, is now

* Matt xv. 13.   † Rev. xxii. 2.
‡ The Danish mythology.   § John iv. 14.

growing on the "Branch" provided for man. The Christian knows the real golden age has not passed; he is looking for its approach, when all faithful souls shall rest under the sheltering "Branch"; when "there shall be no more curse,"* "no night,"† "everlasting joy,"‡ and the whole faithful universe shall exult in the perfected redemption.§ Surely this will be the true golden age, when the "Branch" of the Lord's planting shall spread over all nations!

The Root or Branch of David shall never wither, and will be the only instance of an immortal plant which has grown on earthly soil. It is indeed a contradiction to suppose that the Tree of Life can die. To the end of time its fruit will be for the "healing of the nations," and it will flourish in Paradise by the side of "the Water of Life." When the earth shall be made "new," and shall have become the home of "righteousness,"‖ the "Branch" of the Lord shall be for a beauty and a joy over all who sit in heavenly peace by the "living fountains of waters."¶

This Branch was once visible to men; but to the vast majority, it seemed as "a root out of a dry ground."** Strange that heavenly beauty should attract few eyes, while the deformity of error is deemed beautiful! Men of many lands were enquiring, "Who will shew us any good?"†† An answer was given: the "Branch" of Glory grew

---

* Rev. xxii. 3. † Ib. 5. ‡ Isa. xxxv 10. § Isa. lv. 12; and Rom. viii. 21. ‖ 2 Pet. iii. 13. ¶ Rev. vii. 17. ** Isa. liii. 2. †† Ps. iv. 6.

before them laden with all good, and they knew it
not.

Is not this spiritual blindness hiding the Gospel
fulness still? The world will and must have fruit of
some kind; but they pluck apples of Sodom from
trees of death. The "Branch" is close to every
soul; but a purified eye is required to see the
heavenly fruit, and renewed tastes to desire the
soul's true and everlasting food. In holy quietude
of heart let us rest beneath His sheltering care,
who is both the "root of David" and the "Branch"
of the Lord.

THE LION OF THE TRIBE OF JUDAH.

Rev. v. 5.

When the hosts of liberated Israel were marching
through the desert to the promised land, "the
standard of the camp of the children of Judah"
moved in the van of the great army.* In front of
that divinely-guided march the lion-banner was
carried, as a symbol of the power of the favoured
tribe. Few who looked on that war standard would
then foresee that it would, on a future day, become
the representative of the Messiah. If such a banner
marked out Judah as the chief of all the tribes, the
same symbol may fitly represent Him who is the
hope of all the tribes of the earth. The children of
Judah could boast of a David and a Solomon, but

* Numb. x. 14.

neither of these great leaders could be called "the Lion of the tribe." David knew that his "Lord"* was to be mightier than he, and the words of David's glorious son declared Him "greater than Solomon."† Christ was, indeed, even in His earthly life, the greatest of the royal tribe, and was therefore, in the strictest sense, "the Lion of the tribe." See here another illustration of the truth, that "the Lord seeth not as man seeth." The Jewish historian, Josephus, when desirous of giving the heathen world of his time some exalted notion of the royal family of Judah, speaks of the twenty-one kings of David's line, and tells to the Greeks and Romans the period for which that house held the sceptre, even to the number of the days.‡ But the mightiest name in Judah's regal line is omitted by the Jewish priest, though that name shall outlive all earthly history, and before it "every knee shall bow." To one tribe only of all the varied races of man is Christ related, according to His human nature, and yet a learned man wrote the history of Judah without being conscious of the amazing facts which have made the Saviour of men "the Lion of the tribe of Judah."

This title seems at first to connect our Lord exclusively with one small section of the Jewish people; and does not, therefore, appear suitable for Him who came to live and die, not for Judah only, but for the whole world. Some of the Lord's titles are universal in their bearing, not connecting the Saviour with any particular land, but with the whole

---

* Ps. cx. 1.   † Mat. xii. 42.   ‡ Jos. Antiq. Book x c. 8.

world. No local limitation belongs to such names
as " King of kings," or, " the same yesterday, to-day,
and for ever."   In these, the Redeemer is set forth
as equally related to the entire human race, all distinctions of nationalities disappearing before the
brightness of His divine presence. We contemplate
such universal titles neither as Jews nor as Gentiles,
but as human beings involved in one ruin, and
needing one redemption. But there is a second class
of titles in which Christ has been pleased to associate
Himself, in a peculiar manner, with certain persons
and one special people, or even with one tribe :
" Son of David "—" King of the Jews "—and the
" Lion of the tribe of Judah," are instances of such
local and personal names. As Christ was to be in
all respects like unto men,* so He, of necessity,
selected for Himself human relationships, choosing
for His nation the Jewish people, for His tribe
Judah, and for His family the line of David.   Thus,
while as the Mighty God He makes Himself known
by Divine titles, as " the Son of Man " He has
adopted expressive appellatives from races and from
persons.   Yet who shall say that these people or
individuals have therefore received any special privileges, except the simple honour of furnishing a
title for the Prince of Peace.

Christ permitted Himself to be called " King of
the Jews," but this did not save that people from
utter desolation. He is " the Lion of the tribe of
Judah," but Judah has been a wanderer for eighteen

* Heb. ii. 17.

centuries. The full tide of Gospel blessings surrounds the nations of the West, from whom the Lord has not selected any of His titles.

That the Saviour was, according to the flesh, the greatest and mightiest of the race of Judah is indicated by the title, "Lion of the tribe"; but the image may suggest, at first, ideas not much in harmony with our notions of His boundless love and pity. How can He who died for the world, and who prayed for his murderers, be likened to a lion? As "a lamb" it seems natural to contemplate the ever-blessed Saviour, but can faith consider Him both as a lion and a lamb? Here we have another instance of the amazing variety of characters under which Christ reveals Himself to the Church. No two symbols seem, at the first view, more opposed than a lion and a lamb. Under both the Lord is represented; both must, therefore, be appropriate, and equally full of great truths. In the same heavenly vision He is brought before us under the two forms.* As the "Lion" He alone "prevailed to open" that mysterious book of the seven seals, upon which no created being was able to look; but it is under the form of "a lamb" that He actually took the book. Are not these two, apparently opposed, symbols, descriptive of the opposite works of mercy and judgment which belong to Christ as a Mediator? As a lamb His blood has opened heaven to all believers; but as "the Lion" He will make waste and finally destroy the power of Antichrist. "The

* Rev. v. 5, 6.

wrath of the Lamb"* seems a singular expression;
the idea of a "lamb" and that of "wrath" being so
opposed. Now it is this "wrath of the Lamb"
which finds its proper and natural representation in
the "Lion." As a Saviour rescuing innumerable
multitudes, Christ is the "lamb"; as the destroyer
of long rampant wickedness, He is "the Lion."
Each symbol exactly represents different aspects of
the Lord's work. The great closing contest, when
"all enemies shall be put under His feet,"† brings
the mighty conqueror of death and hell before us as
" the Lion of the tribe of Judah."

There is a peculiar fitness in this image to represent Christ as the destroyer of Satan's power. The
wicked spirit is described as "a roaring lion";‡
now it is not as a lamb the Lord conquers the
ravening beast from the bottomless pit, but as the
Lion of Judah, the appointed messenger of the
Divine judgment.

On the six steps of the ivory throne of Solomon,
twelve lions guarded the approach to the royal seat.§
Thus the symbol of Judah only was associated with
the signs of royalty, and represented all the might
of Israel. So in the work of our redemption, "all
power" is given to "the Lion of the tribe of Judah,"
who alone "prevailed" to open the book of mystery.
As none could approach Solomon on his throne
without first passing by the lions, so no one of the
fallen human race can come to the Eternal Father
except through the Son. The typical lions were

* Rev. vi. 16.   † 1 Cor. xv. 25.   ‡ 1 Pet. v. 8.   § 2 Chron. ix. 18, 19.

a part of the regal state of Solomon, being insepa-
rable from the throne, so Christ, the Lion of Judah,
is at the right hand of the Father, exercising without intermission His mediatorial work.

It is a solemn thought, that every human being
must know Christ either as a lamb or a lion. He
has Himself declared this. He will not only call
"the blessed" of the Father into the everlasting
kingdom, but will certainly drive the impenitent
far away, and even denounce them " as cursed."*
But all true Christians may be blessed by Him
under both characters. To present our whole life
to the Father, relying on the all-sufficient work of
the Son alone, will be to rejoice in Him as " the
Lamb of God." To walk on the road the Lord
points out, though it be over a dreary desert, and
to commit the keeping of our souls to Him, against
all the malice of Satan, is to honour Him as " the
Lion of the tribe of Judah."

THE SON OF MAN.

Matt. viii. 20; xi. 19; xvi. 27; xvii. 22; xviii. 11; xx. 18;
  xxv. 31; xxvi. 2, 24, 45, 64. Mark ii. 10, 28; viii. 38; xiii. 26;
  xiv. 62. Luke xvii. 26, 30. John i. 51; v. 27, &c.

Man's ignorance has formed a subject for speculation, for wonder, or for lamentation, in every age.
Our bodies and our souls are mysteries to us; a leaf
of a tree perplexes us; even a pebble on the road
may baffle the scrutiny of all our science. But far

* Matt. xxv. 34, 46.

above all these cases, in its consequences, is man's
ignorance of his God. When the Creator came so
close to His creature as to unite a human body and
soul to the glorious Godhead; when He talked with
man in man's language; and passed through all the
stages of human life; it seems, at the first view, that
men must surely have learned to know their God.

If Christ be not comprehended as the "Son of
God," He surely will be acknowledged when manifested as the "Son of Man"? If the grandeur of
His Divinity be not seen, the graciousness of His
humanity will be felt? No; ignorance and sin—
two black veils—kept man from worshipping both
the "Son of God," and the "Son of Man."

How completely in all points, sin only excepted,
did the Lord become "like unto us." He might
have created for Himself a human body, and in this
have first appeared in the heavens "with great
glory." But then He would have taken our *form*—
not our nature. Therefore, He was willing to be
born; and we read the marvellous statement, "the
Word was made flesh."* How amazing the contrast, when, as the "Son of God," we see Him
creating all worlds; and then, as the "Son of Man,"
we look upon Him an infant at Bethlehem. Like
man, His human nature passed through all the
stages of childhood and youth, increasing in wisdom
and stature.† A Christian child may be drawn

* John i. 14. For predictions of Christ as "the Son of Man," see
Ps. viii. 4, compared with Heb. ii. 6—8, &c.; 1 Cor. xv. 27. See also
Dan. vii. 13.

† Luke ii. 52.

nearer to Jesus, by remembering that the Saviour
has trodden the path of childhood.

He who created food for more than five thousand
in the wilderness, could at all times have procured miraculous food for Himself; nevertheless, hunger and
thirst were endured* to prove His perfect humanity.
Wonderful is the fact, that, He who is "far above
all principality and power,"† not only felt the
sensation of hunger, but intense, burning thirst on
the cross. He could have removed both the hunger
and the thirst in a moment, yet willingly laid Himself under the load of human suffering, that He
might be like unto men in their bodily trials. The
Heavenly Father permits for a time men to be
tempted by evil spirits, and the "Son of Man"
submitted to receive the assaults of these enemies.
Here is another great mystery of His humanity;
the pure, unspotted "Lamb of God" tempted by
evil angels! Is any one greatly tempted, incessantly
tempted; the Saviour knows your whole case, He
having been "in all points tempted like as we are."‡
The Lord who bade the life-long cripple rise up,§
need never have known fatigue; but we see Him
wearied with His journey, sitting by an ancient
Syrian well for shelter from the mid-day sun.

How clearly does the humanity of the Lord Jesus
appear when He wept. To His mind the death of
Lazarus was foreseen,‖ and the coming destruction
of Jerusalem evident. But when He drew near to

---

* Matt. iv. 2; John xix. 28. † Ephes i. 21. ‡ Heb. iv. 15.
§ John v. 8. ‖ John xi. 4.

the tomb, which for four days had enclosed the
dead; when He saw Mary's tears, and the outpouring of the mourners' grief, then He "was
troubled,"—then "Jesus wept." How thoroughly
human was that sympathy. So when He beheld
Jerusalem filled with a great and rejoicing multitude
from many lands, and saw that, in about forty years,
the proud city would lie in ruinous heaps, He wept
for its blinded population. His own approaching
agony, and the foreseen cruel insults of the Jews,
could not restrain the sympathizing tears of the
" Son of Man."

This deep and wide sympathy belongs to our Lord
now, as fully as when He wept at the tomb of
Lazarus. The more we are able to realize this, the
more shall we trust Him; the more shall we feel the
constraining power of His love.

We know that our Lord's sufferings were not un-
foreseen by Him. The atonement, by a death on the
cross, was pre-determined before the foundation of
the world. But how truly did the humanity of
Christ shew itself by that mysterious pause in the
presence of the coming agony, when He uttered the
words, "If it be possible, let this cup pass from
Me."*

The cup did not pass; Jesus drank it of His own
choice before men and angels; but how natural it
was that His human nature should, if we may so
speak, pause at the beginning of that fearful contest. Every follower of Christ will come to a solemn

* Matt. xxvi. 39.

turn in life's road, where he too must face the king
of terrors. Let us remember that Christ has passed
that very spot; He knows exactly how we feel, as
the moment draws nearer and nearer. His sympathy
is equal to His knowledge; His tenderness is equal
to His power; He will be in the valley just when
most needed.

Two things more were required to make His
human nature like unto ours—death and the grave;
whatever death involves, that the Lord suffered.
The deep silence of the tomb completed the resemblance of His humanity to ours. Like man, He
began His life on earth by a true and proper birth;
like man, He finished by death and a grave. Thus
was He indeed the " Son of Man."

Let us remember that He is the " Son of Man "
amid all the glories of His exaltation; that as " Son
of Man " He will appear visibly before all people;
and that as " Son of Man " He, who was condemned
by the world, will judge the world. Our humanity
is even now glorified in the person of Jesus. "When
He shall appear we shall be like Him,"* and our
raised bodies shall " bear the image " of His
heavenly body.† We are brought wonderfully near
to the eternal Godhead by Him; the everlasting
Word being made flesh, has transformed all
believing children of Adam into heirs and " sons of
God."‡

The wonderful union of the Divine and human
natures in Christ was solemnly taught by Himself.

* 1 John iii. 2.   † 1 Cor. xv. 49.   ‡ Rom. viii. 17 & John i. 12.

In His question to Peter, the Lord adopted the title
expressive of His humanity, and accepted with praise
the disciple's answer acknowledging Him as "the
Son of the living God."*   When the high priest
adjured Jesus to say whether He claimed to be "the
Son of God," the answer was a distinct affirmative ;
but to this was instantly added an equally emphatic
declaration that He was also "the Son of Man."†
Therefore, we believe in Him as "very God of very
God," and also as "the Man Christ Jesus."

* Matt. xvi. 13—17.   † Matt. xxvi. 63, 64.

Section III.

Titles of our Lord

in

HIS DIVINE NATURE.

THE SON OF GOD.
THE BELOVED SON.
THE ONLY BEGOTTEN SON.
THE FIRST BORN OF EVERY CREATURE.
THE IMAGE OF THE INVISIBLE GOD.

THESE five titles bring the Saviour before our view in the glory of His Divinity. As *Son of God* we worship Him, by whom all things were made. *The Beloved Son* declares Him as the object of the Father's mysterious love before the world began. *The Only begotten Son* reminds us of the incomprehensible union which subsisted from everlasting ages between the Eternal Father and the Eternal Son. The *First Born of Every Creature* leads our faith to Him who was " before all things "; and in

The Image of the Invisible God we behold our Lord as the only revealer of the Father; whom no eye hath seen in His pure essential Divinity.

The Son of God.

Matt. iv. 3; viii. 29; xiv. 33; xvi. 16; xxvi. 63, 64; xxvii. 40, 43, 54. Mark i. 1; v. 7. Luke i. 35; xxii. 70. John i. 34; vi. 69. Rom. i. 4.

Some titles of our Lord are easily understood; we can easily comprehend such names as Saviour, Messiah, and King. But others are so bright with a Divine glory, that reasoning is hushed in solemn adoration.

This title, "the Son of God," is one which no "men of understanding"* can explain. Years of deepest thought cannot solve the mystery. An Eternal Father, an Eternal Son, are matters which, perhaps, no created being will ever understand. Can any creature "find out the Almighty unto perfection?"†

Five classes of witnesses have asserted this title of the Saviour. First came the prophets. David, himself a type of the Messiah, foretold the hope of Israel as the Son of God, and even mentions Him as the "begotten," in the words of Jehovah, "this day have I begotten Thee."‡ As "this day," when applied to the ever-living God, can only mean His eternity, so these words teach us that Christ was a

---

* Job xxxiv. 34.   † Job xi. 7.   ‡ Ps. ii. 7, and see Heb. i. 5; v. 5.

son from everlasting ages.* Isaiah calls, by a grand prophetical antithesis, the future Saviour " a child," and also " the mighty God,"† thus comprehending in one short passage the doctrines of the humanity and divinity of the Lord.

Second, the Apostles. They beheld Christ calmly walking where man had never walked before, on the storm-heaving billows of the sea; they marked the ceasing of the tempest as He entered their vessel, and instantly came the confession, " Of a truth Thou art the Son of God." The proof was overwhelming; to have asked " How can it be ?" would have seemed a marvellous impertinence. Thirdly, the Lord Himself claimed to be " the Son of God," before the enraged Jewish council. The assertion was treated as blasphemy by men who were, in their unconscious blindness, condemning their future Judge.‡ We find a fourth class of witnesses to this title in the wicked spirits. Without hesitation these fallen creatures call out, " What have we to do with Thee, Jesus, thou Son of God."§ Strange does it seem that the learned Jewish doctors could not recognize a truth the devils so firmly held. May not a like state of things often exist now ? Men, and learned men too, may be rejecting truths at which the fallen

* In eternity there is neither past nor future, but an everlasting "to-day," was the remark of Luther.

† Isa. ix. 6.

‡ The majority of the Jewish Rabbis had failed to comprehend the lofty teaching of the prophets, and therefore regarded the Lord's claim to be the Son of God, as blasphemy. Matt. xxii. 63—5.

§ Matt. viii. 29.

angels tremble. The holy angels form a fifth class of witnesses. We have, indeed, the words of one only, Gabriel;* but if this pure and bright spirit knew "the Son of God," it is not likely the rest of the heavenly host were left in ignorance. The angels announced the birth of the Saviour, attended Him in the desert,† strengthened Him in the garden of agony,‡ waited at His tomb,§ were present at the ascension,‖ are to aid in assembling the redeemed at the last day,¶ and will accompany Him at the second coming;** it is, therefore, most improbable that beings so honoured should have been ignorant of the Lord's Divine Sonship.

Above eighteen centuries have passed since "the Son of God" walked in a visible form on the earth, but the lapse of ages makes no change in eternal truth. The "Son of God" is now to be confessed by us with the same revering sincerity, as by the disciples of old. Mark the grand result to each one who thus confesses the Son; "God dwelleth in him, and he in God."†† Do we wish to conquer earth? Here is the secret source of power.‡‡ Is the "Son" surrounded with unspeakable glory? a share in that fulness belongs to each one of His followers, for all are reckoned among His "brethren."§§

* Luke i. 35.   ‖ Acts i. 10.   ‡‡ 1 John v. 5.
† Matt. iv. 11.   ¶ Matt. xxiv. 31.   §§ Rom. viii. 29.
‡ Luke xxii. 43.   ** Matt. xxv. 31.
§ John xx. 12.   †† 1 John iv. 15.

THE BELOVED SON.

Matt. iii. 17; xvii. 5. Mark i. 11; ix. 7. Luke iii. 22; ix. 35.

This title of our Lord was proclaimed direct from heaven. Marvellous truths had been spoken through the prophets, glorious things through the apostles, announcements of peace had gone from the heavenly host,* but the Eternal Father Himself revealed this infinite love for His Son. Twice was the expressive declaration uttered; once on the banks of the Jordan, and once on the Mount of the Transfiguration. The multitude of John's proselytes might have heard the first; three apostles only received the second. Each of these mysterious utterances marked important epochs in our Lord's life on earth. The first hallowed His baptism; the second consecrated His Transfiguration.

On each of these occasions impressive celestial signs accompanied the heavenly voices. At the first the opened heavens and the descending symbol of the Holy Spirit marked the Saviour out as the world's great and only perfect Teacher. At the second, how grand were the manifestations. The mighty dead of Israel, her two great human teachers, Moses and Elijah, were there visibly.† Then that "visage so marred"‡ did "shine as the sun," a supernatural light surrounded Him, and the strange

* Luke ii. 14.   † Matt. xvii. 3.   ‡ Isa. lii. 14.

brightness of the cloud "overshadowed" the amazed disciples.

Three of the evangelists have recorded these Divine proclamations and their accompanying signs, and this title of the Redeemer is, doubtless, specially set forth for our contemplation. What *perfect* satisfaction does the Father express in those words :— "My beloved Son, in whom I am *well pleased.*" "The heavens are not clean in His sight,"* and "His angels He charged with folly,"† but He looks on His Son with an infinite approbation. Let us remember that the Son had always been "beloved"; long before the foundation of the world,‡ before any being was created, or before "the morning stars sang together."§

This mysterious relationship of the Father to the Son is, of course, incomprehensible by us ; but in what a light does it place the love of the Father to men. To accomplish our redemption this "beloved Son" was appointed, ere time began,‖ to undergo sufferings of which we can form no conception. Often let us contemplate this great mystery, which is a stronger argument than even the Creation itself to prove that "God is love."

The Father has condescended to reveal to us His love for the Son ; and the question arises, "How do we regard that Son?" Are His offers of mercy received, His love prized, His atonement trusted, and has He become our *all* for time and for eternity ?

* Job. xv. 15.   † Job. iv. 18.   ‡ John xvii. 24.
§ Job. xxxviii. 7.   ‖ 1 Pet. i. 20.

THE ONLY-BEGOTTEN SON.

John i. 18; iii. 16.

The sons of God by creation form a vast multitude; the sons of God by adoption shall be a glorious host; but we find one only who is called the "Only-begotten Son of God." Here we approach a great mystery; speculation is useless, reasoning vain; we have only to listen to the wonderful revelation, and to adore. The sonship of our Lord will perhaps remain for ever far above the comprehension of all created understandings. The Saviour is a Son in a most peculiar sense; each of the three words, "Only-begotten Son," is encirled by a mysterious glory. Before a star was created—before any angel existed, when all this wondrous universe had a shape in the Divine mind only, even then the Son was in the bosom of the Father, rejoicing in the fulness of uncreated majesty.* When the worlds came into being at the Divine word, the "only-begotten Son" joined in the wondrous work.† In the mighty workings of the adorable Father, the Son has ever co-operated,‡ and the frame of creation is even now kept in harmony by Him.§

That such a Son should be the "beloved;" that "all fulness" should dwell in Him;‖ that He should "be equal with" the Father;¶ that He should receive like honour;** that He shall be the Judge

---

* John xvii. 5, 24.   † John i. 3.   ‡ John v. 17.   § Col. i. 17.
‖ Col. i. 19.   ¶ Phil. ii. 6.   ** John v. 23.

of mankind,* and receive the worship of all
creation,† we might have expected. But that the
" only-begotten Son " should mysteriously lay aside
the unspeakable glories which He enjoyed before
the creation of the world, become acquainted with
human suffering, live with prejudiced and ignorant
men, and suffer, of His own free will, a most
ignominious death, are events which could have
entered into no imagination of man or angel. No
one would dare to believe such marvels possible,
had not the Father and the Son both joined in
revealing them. Do we wish for some deep and
clear exposition of the words, " God is love ?" then
surely the humiliation of the " only-begotten Son "
is the brightest comment we can have. Are we
sometimes, when we lose sight for a moment of
grand Bible principles, led to doubt of the Divine
love, amidst the terrible calamities and sins which
often darken the earth ? Reflect, then, on that
grandest of all facts, the gift of the " only-begotten
Son !" The love that accomplished such a result
may be safely trusted. What can be withheld,
after such a gift has been so freely bestowed ?‡
Ask everything therefore from the Father, through
the Son; and murmur not at the manner or the
form in which Divine love sends the answer.

What a mysterious depth of evil must belong to
sin, when nothing less than the sufferings of the
" only-begotten Son " could open a path of escape !
The earth, indeed, is a volume in which may be

* John v. 22.   † Phil. ii. 10.   ‡ Rom. viii. 32.

read the miseries of sin; the desolations, agonies, and passions of war; public frauds, and wide-spread social selfishness; and the withering influence of sin in thousands of private homes. Had these results been experienced but in one country, for one century only, the scene might have filled an angel's heart with grief. But the venom of sin has not become exhausted by a continued action for six thousand years, or by diffusion over the whole earth. To all this, add the misery which awaits rebellious man in the life to come. Such results must startle the most unthinking! We may judge of the cause by the terrible nature of the effects;—of the malignancy of the disease by the severity of the symptoms. A mysterious plague had broken out in the world—how could it be checked? Many remedies had been tried; philosophy had reasoned; moralists had entreated; and legislators commended; but the world became rather worse.

At length, the fearful mystery of sin was met by the heavenly mystery of redemption. The "only-begotten Son" descended to destroy the works of the Devil;* and this, not by magnificent, visible conquests over the powers of darkness, but by suffering and death. This amazing gift from the Father gives a peculiar grandeur to the history of this earth. There may be other worlds inhabited by a higher race of beings; but there is no intimation that for any of them the "only-begotten Son" has been given. May we not, with deepest

* 1 John iii. 8.

reverence, now say, that upon us the eternal Father
has conferred His *mightiest* gift? Love, wisdom,
and power, all the riches of the Godhead, seem
concentrated in this bestowal of the "only Son."
The great spiritual triumph is secured, the "times
of refreshing" are approaching; when the "new
heavens and the new earth" shall acknowledge this
marvellous and mysterious gift to be the highest,
fullest, and everlasting proof of the Father's love!

THE FIRST-BORN OF EVERY CREATURE.

Col. i. 15.

This title of the Lord makes us conscious of the
impenetrable mysteries, the clouds and darkness
which surround the eternal throne. We can easily
receive the statement that our blessed Saviour was,
according to His human nature, the "first-born
Son" of the Virgin; but the understanding feels
confounded by the idea presented in the words,
"the First-born of every Creature." Even when
the words, "the First-begotten of all Creation,"*
have been substituted for our authorized translation,
the mind is no nearer to a comprehension of the
mystery. We can see in such language the glorious,
the unspeakable pre-eminence, which it is the Father's
good pleasure the Son should possess. To impress
this idea on our minds, the deeply significant terms,

---

* πρωτότοκος πάσης κτίσεως.

"Only-begotten"—"the First-begotten of all Creation"—"Begotten before the Worlds"—and similar
exalting epithets are employed. The great result,
thus enforced, being that all men should "honour
the Son, even as they honour the Father." The
Saviour is therefore exalted in view of the whole
universe, that to Him the loftiest and the deepest
homage of creation should be paid. How appropriate is the honour thus decreed to "the Son of
His love"* by the everlasting Father! He who
was "lifted up" on the Cross, who was exposed to
the contempt of the world's great ones, is now far
"above all principality and power." Let us mark
how the apostle, enrapt by the grandeur of the
subject, draws out the magnificent argument. He
first contemplates the agony by which "redemption,
through His blood," was purchased;† then, turning
from that solemn scene of the Saviour's humiliation,
he beholds Jesus as "the invisible God," and as
"the First-begotten of all Creation." At this point
the apostle pauses to shew *why* the Redeemer must
be thus regarded. "For by Him were all things
created,"‡ are the words which force us to regard
our great Atoner as placed at the head of the whole
universe. Mark the successive stages of glory
presented to us in that wonderful passage,§ every
word of which is bright with a heavenly light, and
laden with such a weight of spiritual thought, that
the Christian heart can only ponder in solemn

* τοῦ υἱοῦ τῆς ἀγάπης αὐτοῦ—Col. i. 13.   † Col. i. 14.
‡ Col. i. 16.   § Col. i. 15 to 18.

silence over the sublime mystery! No passage in
the whole range of Scripture sets before us a more
exalting epitome of our Lord's pre-eminence. The
invisible world seems laid open to our view; the
thrones, dominions, principalities, and powers, all
rise before us as subjects of our Heavenly King;
for "all were created by Him, and for Him."
The heart almost shrinks from contemplating such
a rich and incomprehensible concentration of glory
and honour. But we must not shut our eyes to the
Saviour's exaltation, or we shall never understand
the value of His humiliation, and the unspeakable
merits of His perfect sacrifice. Let us try to realize
the truths respecting the Divine nature and mediatorial glory of our ever-blessed Lord. Unless we
attain to lofty views of Christ, our estimate of
redemption will have a narrowness, which will surely
check the development of the Christian life.

He, who thus stands at the head of the visible
and invisible creation; who created "all things;"
by whose ever-present energy, "all things consist,"
and are preserved in their beautiful and harmonious
action,—He must be God. Wonderful is the gradual
ascent by which the Holy Spirit, in the Scripture,
conducts our faith, and also our enlightened and
disciplined reason! We see the Saviour at the
beginning, "the first-born" of the Virgin Mary;
we then trace His mysterious life through its stages
of teaching, temptation, working, and suffering,
until we pause, in awe, before the Cross and the
Lamb. We are then called to follow the victorious

Saviour triumphing over the grave, ascending as "the Forerunner" of a countless multitude to that Holy of Holies, the consecrated glory of which no mortal eye can see. But faith, aided by the Holy Ghost, still follows the Lord into the inner mansions of the heavens, and beholds Him, "the first-begotten of all Creation," ruling the thrones, dominions, and principalities. When the Christian has thus been enabled to apprehend the exaltation of his Lord, he feels and sees the force of the title, "the First-born (first-begotten) of all creation." He sees that the words place before him the *pre-eminence* of Christ, not only as "Head of the Church," but of the whole universe. The first-begotten is the "appointed heir of all things,"* and, therefore, the whole created system, with its starry families extending far beyond the reach of the most penetrating telescope—all are His. But this Mighty One, this "blessed and only potentate,"† is the Saviour to whom we have committed the keeping of our souls for time and for eternity. Well, therefore, may each Christian rejoice in the full persuasion that he is able to keep that which "I have committed unto Him."‡

The angels sang a hymn of joy when the Father brought "the first-begotten into the world,"§ and surely the whole redeemed family of God should rejoice, when contemplating the exaltation of Him who loved them and gave Himself for them, and who is now as "the first-begotten of all creation," exercising His unlimited power for their salvation.

* Heb. i. 2.   † 1 Tim. vi. 15.   ‡ 2 Tim. i. 12.   § Heb. i. 6.

E

THE IMAGE OF THE INVISIBLE GOD.

Colossians i. 15.

The signs of an invisible presence surround us on
every hand. The thoughtful and religious mind sees
in the unfolding leaf the working of a mysterious
power. Every movement in nature—the passing
breeze stirring the forest foliage, the ebb and flow
of the ocean waters, and the noiseless motion of
the starry hosts, all speak of His wonderful nearness, by whom they live, and move, and have their
being. But has the mighty Creator ever made
Himself visible? "No man hath seen God at any
time,"* is the answer. The pillar of fire which
shone so wondrously through the darkness of the
desert,† and cast its supernatural light over the
troubled waters of the Red Sea, was but a *sign* of
the Divine presence. Even that strange light of
the Shechinah, which at times filled the tabernacle
with a marvellous brightness,‡ descended as "the
glory of the Lord" on the first temple,§ and was
supposed to rest, a solemn witness of God, on the
mercy-seat between the cherubim,—even this was
but a symbol of the Lord's nearness.‖ Isaiah, in
his magnificent and humbling vision, beheld only

---

* John i. 18. † Exod. xiii. 21. ‡ Exod. xl. 34, 38. § 2 Chron. v. 14.
‖ The word Shechinah, from Shaucan "He dwelt," was used by the
Rabbins to denote the visible symbol of Deity.

some glorious signs of Jehovah's presence;* God had not been seen. Yet there is a sense in which the unseen has been made visible, for the Lord from heaven is "the Image of the invisible God." The Divine Son has tabernacled among men, and in Him mankind have seen the everlasting Father,† whose "express image "‡ has thus been manifested to us.

As our Holy Redeemer is "the Image of the invisible God," His life on earth must have been a clear revelation of the Divine attributes, so far as man could bear the manifestation. "*Power* belongeth unto God,"§ is a doctrine of Scripture, and the teaching of universal nature. This peculiar excellence of the Almighty was fully possessed by the Saviour. The "invisible God" hides the full working of His wondrous energy behind the veil of natural laws and daily phenomena; but the Son, as His "image," has set visibly before men the marvels of creative and preserving power. When the earth first rose into being, with all its rich and varied beauty, man beheld not this manifestation of glory. "The morning stars sang together," but the grandeur of the new creation was witnessed by angels only. The time came, however, when the loving Father of spirits sent His Son to be unto mankind an "image" of the perfections of the Godhead. Then human eyes saw even *creative* power exerted visibly on the earth. The Lord did not indeed create a world; His manifestation of Godlike power was suited to the perceptions and wants of His feeble creatures;

* Isaiah vi. 1—4. † John xiv. 9. ‡ Heb. i. 3. § Psalm lxii. 11.

and, therefore, the Saviour shewed His Divine power
by creating, in the space of a few minutes, and
before the eyes of above five thousand hungry
people, bread and fish more than sufficient for that
multitude.* The wondering host, seated in the cool
of the evening on the grass in the desert, beheld as
decisive an act of creation as did the angels when
they saw the new world rise up in the freshness of
its primal beauty. In another miracle the old substance was changed into a new—water became wine ;
the conversion being a decisive result of that power
over matter, which we properly call creative. In
these manifestations of all controling might, our
Redeemer was " The Image of the invisible God."

The loving kindness of the Father, the inconceiv-
able pity of the Most High God for His fallen and
wandering children were also seen in " His Image."
The widow of Nain is alone on the earth, alone in
the midst of a mourning procession ; on the bier lies
her only son, silent in the deep solemn calm of
death ; tears, such as death alone can wring from
stricken hearts, are falling ; and the trembling,
bereaved woman may be fearing that even God has
forsaken her. But in that hour of her agony, the
Father sent His Son Christ as " the Image of the
invisible God," and He looked upon the mourner.
How cold, how stoical His first words must have
sounded, " Weep not." When shall she weep if not
now ? But the calmness of the Saviour was but the
mysterious quietude of Divine power united with

* Matt. xiv. 15—21.

Divine pity; for "He had compassion on her"!
What a mysterious touch that bier then felt; how
strangely solemn must have seemed the pause of the
funeral procession; how utterly amazing the up-
rising and the speaking of him who had just before
been "a dead man"; and what a fulness of Divine
pity did the Lord exhibit, when, with His own
hands, He delivered the restored one to "his
mother."* Surely here Jesus was in truth "the
Image of the invisible God."

The whole life of Christ on earth was but the
visible representation—"the image" of those glorious
attributes under which it has pleased the Father to
make Himself known to mankind. The Divine
knowledge of man's secret thoughts was seen in
the Saviour, when His understanding detected
the unuttered reasonings of the Scribes;† perfect
fore-knowledge was shown in the delineation of
the incidents connected with the future siege of
Jerusalem ; ‡ forbearance and longsuffering were
manifested in the forgiveness of Peter and the
prayer for His murderers; and His right to Divine
honour was indicated by His acceptance of the name
of "God" from the repentant Thomas. The whole
series of incidents connected with the work of our
Saviour, shew Him to be the "Image of the
invisible God."

Moses, the prophets, and the apostles, performed
many wonderful works, by God working in them ;

* Luke vii. 11—15.   † Matt. ix. 4.
‡ Matt. xxiv. 2, 15 ; Luke xix. 43, 44 ; xxi. 20, 24.

but none of these divinely-honoured men so represented their God as to be called His "Image."
That peculiar honour belonged to the Son only,
who having been from eternity with God, and being
Himself God,* could alone be to a world of fallen
men an "Image" of the Most Holy.

We are thus presented with another of those most
startling contrasts which abounded in the life of our
Lord.   God in great goodness allowed mankind to
behold His "Image" in the Son.   The nations
endeavoured utterly to destroy and to cover with
infamy the representation of their Creator.   The
names of mere mortals were engraven on marble in
many a stately temple; the idols of the east and of
the west were honoured, but "the Image of the
invisible God" was "despised and rejected."

But most glorious is the vision which this title of
the Son brings before a Christian eye.   Man was
made in "the image of God"; the Lord of Life has
appeared on earth bearing "the image" of man's
Maker; and all believers in Christ Jesus shall be
restored in Him to "the image of the heavenly."†
What a mysterious circle of life will then be completed.   The beginning was in sinless beauty; the
early course was distorted by the Fall; the war of
light and darkness perplexed age after age; the
descent of the Son from the eternal mansions has
revealed the glories of the Godhead in human form;
and the wondrous end is coming, when the whole
multitude of the saved "shall be like Him,"‡ who is
"the Image of the invisible God."

* John i. 1.   † 1 Cor. xv. 49.   ‡ 1 John iii. 2.

———◆———

Titles of our Lord

AS

THE WORLD'S GREAT TEACHER.

———◆———

THE GREAT PROPHET.
THE WORD.
THE WORD OF LIFE.
THE TRUTH.
THE TEACHER COME FROM GOD.
THE TRUE LIGHT.
THE LIGHT OF THE WORLD.
THE BRIGHT AND MORNING STAR.

THESE eight titles exhibit our all-wise Lord as the source of Divine instruction. He is truly *The Prophet* who is the end and origin of all prophecy. As *The Word,* He reveals the deep counsels of the Father; and as *The Word of Life,* brings into the world the only life-giving doctrines. "*The Truth*" is beautifully descriptive of Him in whom all truth

centres, and to whom it leads. *The Teacher come
from God* proclaims Him the bearer of the Father's
great and peculiar commission. *The True Light*
shews Him in contrast with the many false lights of
time. *The Light of the World* predicts the spread
of His Gospel among all people; and, as *The Bright
and Morning Star,* He shines from His heavenly
height, the only true Guide of the wandering human
race.

THE GREAT PROPHET.

John vii. 40; iv. 19; vi. 14. Luke vii. 16; xxiv. 19.

The Saviour was not only foretold under the
comprehensive title of the Messiah, which by itself
reminds us of His three great offices, but was also
announced to the ancient Church by the special
names of Priest,* King,†, and Prophet. Moses
when about to die, described to the tribes of Israel
the coming of one who should be to them a new
law-giver and a new teacher. "Like unto me,"
was the description given fifteen hundred years
before the Lord appeared as the great Prophet of
His people. "I will put my words in His mouth,"
was the declaration of the eternal Father respecting
the future infallible teacher; "unto Him shall ye
hearken," was the injunction then given to the
Jews, and now laid upon all to whom the Gospel
comes.‡

* Psalm cx. 4.   † Psalm ii. 6.
‡ Deut. xviii. 15—18; Acts iii. 22, 23; vii. 37.

Isaiah foresaw the Lord exercising His prophetical office as the preacher of " good tidings " and the proclaimer of " liberty to the captives."* After nearly eight hundred years this very prediction was read in the Synagogue at Nazareth by the foretold " Prophet," who applied to Himself in the hearing of the wondering congregation, the words of ancient prophecy.†

The multitude for awhile gladly received Him as " the Prophet of Nazareth,"‡ as " a great Prophet," as " the Prophet that should come,"§ and the malicious chief priests were compelled for a short time to respect the popular voice.‖ The Apostles, even after their Master's crucifixion, described Him as " a Prophet mighty in deed and in Word."¶ Even the woman of Samaria, notwithstanding the dimness of her spiritual perception, could perceive the prophetic glory in the wearied stranger, who sitting by the ancient well had touched her heart by His words.** The blind man, who had received at the same time the two gifts of natural and spiritual sight, condensed all his thankful reverence in the words " He is a Prophet."††

The Lord is the Great Prophet in a high and comprehensive sense, for it was " the Spirit of Christ "‡‡ which testified in each of the long line of inspired seers. Every prediction was therefore a revelation, not by the prophet who spoke the words,

* Isaiah lxi. 1. § Luke vii 16 ; John vi. 14. ** John iv. 19.
† Luke iv 16—21. ‖ Matt. xxi. 46. †† John ix. 17.
‡ Matt. xxi. 11. ¶ Luke xxiv. 19. ‡‡ 1 Pet. i. 11.

but by Him who has ever been, and is, the wisdom
of God.*   Thus the anointed One was truly a
Prophet to His Church from the beginning of the
world.   No marvel, therefore, that all "the prophets"† point to Christ, who is to be found, not in
a few isolated passages, but clearly traced by a
continuous line of holy light, through the long roll
of prophecy. This was to be expected. It was not
probable that a revelation from heaven should put in
the back ground of prophecy, such wonders as the
incarnation, the sacrifice, and mediatorial glory of
the eternal Son.   Christ, whose Spirit had given the
revelation, and who knew the fulness of the predictions concerning Himself, assured the Jews that the
whole body of the Scriptures testified of Him.‡

No text of the Bible must be wrested, no passage
fancifully interpreted, but all who remember that
the patriarchs beheld from afar the glory of the
Redeemer ;§ that "the law was our schoolmaster to
bring us unto Christ,"‖ and that from the most
ancient to the latest prophetical book, predictions of
the coming salvation occur in the varied forms of
literal description, vision, type, and symbol,—will
expect to hear their Saviour speaking in every part
of the Old Testament. Thus the Lord was Himself
the Great Prophet of the first dispensation, and
through an eventful period of nearly four thousand
years, was preparing the world for His manifestations

---

* 1 Cor. i. 24.   § Gen. xlix. 10; John viii. 56.
† Acts x. 43.   ‖ Gal. iii. 24.
‡ John v. 39.

in human form. During this long era He seldom became visible even to His most honoured servants, but when the fulness of time came, all the rays of prophetic light were centred in Him as the Great Prophet of the Father, the world, and the Church.

As we have but one true and everlasting Priest, one Almighty, ever-present King, so there is but one all-wise Prophet. Before His coming, the lamp of prophecy was held up by merely human hands, but when the true Sun arose in brightness, the earthen lamps were laid aside. Never again shall an Isaiah depict the future glory of the Messiah; no more will a Daniel write the chronology of future ages; the Great Prophet has spoken and all other voices are hushed. Some may think it strange that such a teacher should have left no writings of His own for the guidance of disciples in every age. Some credulous Christians of the fourth century may for awhile have believed in the existence of a few such documents,* but He who was "the wisdom of God" saw fit to intrust His life-giving words to honest-hearted and simple-minded men, whom He selected to live with Him for the space of three years. To them the Great and Infallible Prophet made known the mysteries of heaven in some degree while He was with them; in still higher measure after His

---

* As the short letter to Abgarus, King of Edessa in Mesopotamia, mentioned with doubt by the historian Eusebius; the idle *rumour* of two other letters of Christ referred to by Augustine, who died 530 A.D. A small sect of heretics in the fourth century even ventured to trace one of their hymns to Christ.

departure. His Spirit had spoken in the prophets
of the old dispensation, and the same Spirit guided
"into all truth"* the Apostles of the more spiritual
age. The heavenly treasures were indeed put into
earthen vessels, but the vessels were of Christ's own
choosing, and made fit to convey to the Church the
gifts they received. One alone was broken,† and
left as a warning to the faithless of all ages. The
followers of Christ have not therefore suffered loss,
though their Great Prophet did in His wisdom
withhold writings of His own; for He gave to the
Apostles "the words" which the Father had given
to Him.‡ How emphatically solemn were some of
those predictions which Christ, as the anointed
Prophet, uttered in the hearing of the Jewish people.
The swiftly-approaching ruin of Jerusalem was set
before its irritated and startled inhabitants with all
the distinctness of a picture, traced in lines of supernatural light. The Roman trench, the heathen
standards, the encompassing armies, the ruined
temple, the desolate city, the false Christs, and the
captive population, were set vividly before the men
of that generation.§ Within forty years after the
utterance of the prediction, all came to pass, and
some who had heard the prophetic warning may
have witnessed its fulfilment.‖ Still the scattered
Jews keep the annual fast, which, whilst it reminds
them of the destruction of their ancient temple, is

---

* John xvi. 18.   † Iscariot.   ‡ John xvii. 8.
§ See Matt. xxiii. 38; xxiv. 2, 5, 15; Luke xix. 43, 44; xxi. 20, 24.
‖ Titus took Jerusalem in the year 70 A.D.

also a witness for His truth who came as a prophet to their fathers.

Is not the whole Church waiting now for the accomplishment of another prediction of far wider significance and deeper import than that which related to Jerusalem? The Great Prophet will become visible once more, and has left for our meditation and warning, a prophetic description of that wonderful event.* Working, watching, and waiting are now the duties of the Church; and in all these the heart will be strengthened by frequent contemplation of those predictions of His second coming, which the greatest of all prophets has left to quicken faith, hope, and love.

The Anointed Prophet of the Father, though foretold through a long succession of ages, was rejected by many of those who even heard His searching words and beheld his marvellous works. His teaching is still neglected, His miracles misunderstood. Many are calling for more evidence; but more candour, more honesty of heart, more love of truth, more freedom from prejudice, are the real wants.

Multitudes have, however, learned to understand and trust the teaching of the only perfect Prophet. They see His teaching in many an ancient rite, they hear His voice in the prophetic books, and are now expecting with a humble and hallowing joy, the accomplishment of the glorious predictions which have quickened the hearts of the faithful in every age.

* Matt. xxv. 31—46.

THE WORD.

John i. 1 ; 1 John v. 7 ; Rev. xix. 13.

The deepest thoughts of a man are made evident
to the whole world by words. Nothing is more
invisible than thought, nothing more silent; but
clothe it in a word, and it shall be visible to millions,
and speak with a voice which may be heard through
long ages. The words of Milton are but the thoughts
of Milton made visible in beautiful and artistic forms;
thus, words are our mode of revealing a man's inner
life to his fellow men.

How fitly then is Christ called "The Word," for
by Him the eternal Father has declared his everlasting counsels to mankind. "No man hath seen
God at any time,"* is the solemn declaration of Holy
Scripture, and the proud Jews were reminded that
they had never heard the Father's "voice at any
time," or "seen His shape."† Then whose voice
did Adam hear in the garden?‡ To whom did
Abraham address that wonderful prayer for the
doomed city?§ Whose voice was heard from Sinai
by the awe-stricken Jews?‖ All these wonderful
manifestations must have been made by the Son,
who, as the Word, declared the Father's purposes.¶

This great truth was not hidden from the Jews of
old, who constantly ascribe to "The Word of God"

---

* John i. 18.   ‡ Gen. iii. 8.   ‖ Exod. xx. 19.
† John v. 37.   § Gen. xviii. 23—33.   ¶ John i. 18.

the glorious manifestations of Divine power recorded in the Old Testament.*

Through all ages, "The Word" has revealed the hidden things of God unto the Church. The prophets beheld visions of mercy and of judgment, but this was through the "Spirit of Christ which was in them."† The company of the Apostles have spoken to us "the wisdom of God," but they first received the precious truths from Him who alone had seen the Father."‡

Let us endeavour to realize the great truth, that God the Father manifests His glory to man through The Word only. What an evangelical significance this gives to everything round us. The Christian astronomer cannot examine the remote depths of the starry universe, without remembering that not one of these distant worlds came into being without the co-operation of The Word.§ When the man of science marks the stability of the vast system, he will recollect that by "The Word" all things consist.|| The politician, who is perplexed by the sounds of coming strife, may be calmed by remembering that "all things" are under the feet of Jesus, The Divine Word.¶ Thus we find that, in Creation, Providence, and Redemption, the mighty God, whom "no man hath seen, nor can see," has manifested His glory through Him who is therefore beautifully and truly called "The Word."

---

* See Pearson on the Creed, Art. ii. pp. 178—9.

† 1 Pet. i. 11.   § Col. i. 16.   ¶ Eph. i. 22.

‡ John vi. 46. || Col. i. 17.

THE WORD OF LIFE.

1 John i. 1.

The words of death are often heard and read. Every published falsehood, all promulgated irreligion, produce fatal results to multitudes. The writer of one profane book kills the souls of men, not only in his own age, but continues to destroy long after he has been buried. We may suppose the case of one such writer becoming conscious, in the light of the next world, of all his published wickedness, and trembling at the consequences of the mischief working on the earth in his name. How terrible is the punishment of Mahommed, if, from the world of spirits, he now sees the moral desolation produced by his audacious fiction! If the words of death thus work among the successive generations of mankind, are there any words of life to counteract and to overcome the deadly energy of evil? There are words spoken by men " of old time," words of beauty and words of power, which the nations gratefully cherish. But do they impart life? No; such words do not come from earth, or from the children of the earth.

" The Word of Life " has been amongst men; the eternal Logos (Word) who " was with God," and " was God," has been heard speaking to mankind; and, therefore, we have hopes that the words of death shall yet be hushed. When the wonderful

command, "Lazarus come forth," was uttered, the
amazed crowd saw before them "The Word of Life"
manifesting His power in the territories of the dead.
His glory, as the life producing Word, had been
witnessed, probably, by worshipping angels, long
before Lazarus heard His voice.   By this Word all
things were made,* and we cannot therefore look up
to the heavens, or gaze on the diversified beauty of
earth, without being reminded of our Saviour as "The
Word of Life."   The day of creation was indeed a
mysterious manifestation of His divine glory.

There shall come another day of wonder when, at
the voice of "The Word of Life," the innumerable
dead shall rise, receiving immortal vigour from the
glorified Saviour.

"The Word of Life" has manifested His divine
power in producing a more important result than
even the creation of the world or the resurrection of
the body.   What real beauty would belong to the
material universe if it were the home of rebellious
spirits ?   Would the resurrection be a matter for joy
if all that raised multitude were wicked ?   Better to
have slept in the dust of the earth for ever, than to
awake to shame and suffering. "The Word of Life"
has become the author of that spiritual resurrection,
by which souls are quickened, and every power of the
heart filled with a holy energy.   This is the true life
of a created being, the endowment which saves him
from ranking with the demons, and fits him for the
companionship of the spirits of light.   This is the

* John i. 3.

gift upon which Christ would fix our gaze when
calling Himself " the bread of life." To open a way
for the full and free grant of this heavenly boon was
the object of all the amazing humiliations, sufferings,
and death of " The Word of Life." What a contrast
does this suggest between the Son of God as Creator
and Redeemer. He made all things by the word of
His power; He spake, and it was done. Creation,
speaking according to our modes of thought, was
an easy work. But before " The Word of Life "
could accomplish the redemption of man, it was
*necessary** that the " only-begotten " and " well-
beloved Son " should pass through a series of sorrows too peculiar for us at present to comprehend.
Surely the life thus purchased must far exceed in
importance the simple result of creative power.
Christ, therefore, as the purchaser, the origin, and
the supporter of our renewed nature, is fitly called
" The Word of Life."

The regeneration of the soul by a Divine call only,
is often clearly brought within the range of our
experience.   One man possesses knowledge wide
and various, is deeply and critically acquainted with
Scripture, appreciating its beauties and interested
in its history, listening constantly to eloquent appeals
and forcible arguments, and yet this man shall never
feel a true repentance, never know a saving faith.
Another may be truly classed among the uneducated,
and, in comparison with the former, be a very child
in intellect, yet the latter may receive the offers of

* Luke xxiv. 26.

mercy, and obey from the heart "The Word of Life." An *impression* has been made on the one heart to which the other is a stranger. "This is the Lord's doing, and it is marvellous," must be the natural conclusion of those who trace effects to their causes.

"The Word of Life" when admitted into the soul, seems in all cases to produce that consciousness of the unseen world and that sense of the Divine presence so rare among men.

This susceptibility to impressions is a marked sign of natural life. To see, to hear, to feel, prevent the question of death arising. What answers to these senses in spiritual life ? Is it not that faith which is " the evidence of things not seen,"* under which the soul feels the invisible God to be near, rejoices in the presence of an unseen Saviour, and becomes more mindful of its position as one of that family which belongs to both heaven and earth. Under such influences all things are gradually estimated by a new standard. Life and death; time and eternity; the body and the soul; the true nature of sin; the wants and capacities of the heart; the life of Christ; the influence of the Holy Spirit; the doctrine of Providence; the past, the present, and the future of earth; all these points are viewed in a new light. No wonder that such a change is represented as a passing from " death unto life." How admirably does the title " The Word of Life," describe the author of this great and critical renewal. Well is Christ called " Our Life," since, as the

* Heb. xi. 1.

eternal Word, He created us; as our sacrifice, He redeemed us; and as our Mediator, procures the daily grace which prepares for endless glory.

What then remains, but to listen with reverent ear to those heavenly intimations, and to receive with grateful hearts the supplies of strength, which in His loving wisdom "The Word of Life" will assuredly give to all true disciples.

THE TRUTH.

John xiv. 6.

Truth is praised, but falsehood is followed. Every man professes to be the friend of truth; yet the vast majority are found on the side of error. Large audiences can be roused into passionate excitement by descriptions of the beauty and grandeur of truth, though seven-tenths of the individuals composing that mass may be clinging to some delusion.

This contradiction between conscience and practice is not peculiar to any age or nation. The refined Roman poet, though a pagan, felt and acknowledged the fatal opposition, saying, "I see and acknowledge what is good, but I follow what is evil."* The conscience of the whole human race would doubtless

* *Ovid's* Confession, " Video meliora proboque deteriora sequor."

express itself in similar language, did not conscience itself often become seared or blind.

If truth be in the world, why does it not triumph? Men say that "great is the truth, and it shall prevail;" but how can it be victorious, when against it are arrayed all the weaknesses, the prejudices, the ignorance, and the vices of mankind? Who can clearly distinguish truth? Some falsehoods walk abroad dressed in white, and men ask in perplexity, or in scorn, "What is truth?"

Lay aside your fears, and receive an answer from the Lord of men and angels, who declares Himself to the world as "The Truth." Others may have taught *a* truth, or *some* truths, but the Redeemer proclaims Himself, without limitation, as "The Truth." Patriarchs and prophets taught truths; but Christ *is* truth: note His remarkable words, "I *am* the Truth."

We are thus reminded that the Bible contains but one great doctrine, the centre of the whole system of revelation, "Jesus Christ, the same yesterday, to-day, and for ever."* Around this all Scripture history, prophecy, doctrine, and precepts revolve. The apostle thoroughly apprehended this, when he said, "We preach Christ crucified;"† he does not enumerate a series of doctrines, but considers them all to be comprehended in "The Truth." When churches, when individual Christians feel this, their spiritual life is safe: when they cannot realize it, inevitable decline follows. In vain, there are creeds,

* Heb. xiii. 8.   † 1 Cor. i. 23.

learning, wealth, and splendour: the Shechinah is not in them. The truth must, without doubt, be *pure;* "nothing but the truth." The Gospel cannot be corrected; the pure gold cannot be made purer. Science, learning, and criticism may remove the dust which has accumulated and concealed the purity of the metal, but no refiner's furnace is wanted. Churches may need reformation, but not the Lord's words; Christian communities may admit of development, but "The Truth" was perfect from the beginning. We hear many complaints now of the untruthfulness of the age, of its tendency to shams and showy pretences. If these charges be correct, the age can only be corrected by coming under the influence of principles which destroy falsehoods in every form.

This title of the Lord bids us remember that His doctrine was *all divine.* Part was not collected from human schools and part from heaven. All proceeded from Him, as "The Truth." Men speak of "Christianity as old as the creation;" they have spoken truly, though undesignedly. Adam did, undoubtedly, hear the grand truth which makes the Gospel;* and the message of Divine mercy is therefore ancient; but it descended from heaven. The Church of Christ is called "the pillar and ground of the truth," as she holds it up before the world; but she did not originate a single doctrine, though she receives all. "The Truth" gave life to the Church, not the Church to "The Truth."

* Gen. iii. 15,

Christ being so emphatically "The Truth," must be peculiarly *adapted* to satisfy the human heart. Man is remarkable for the number of his wants; and the poet was certainly mistaken when he wrote, "Man wants but little here below." Men are often ignorant of their greatest needs; but when the soul feels and sees the nature and extent of her dangers, she will no longer be appeased by the old shams and lying vanities. She requires not only truth, but truth adapted to her feeble, sinful, and ignorant state. It may safely be affirmed that not one human spirit can be found to whose wants "The Truth" is unsuited. It matters little whether the man be a philosopher, rivalling the fame of Newton, or a red Indian, ignorant of the alphabet; the exact fitness of "The Truth" to the wants of each will be the same. Each man resembles his fellow-man in all his great necessities; the emperor and the beggar alike needing renewal of heart, pardon, the daily help of the Holy Spirit, and perfect acceptance in Christ.

This fitness of the Gospel to meet all our spiritual wants may not be felt, just as the beautiful adaptation of light to the human eye cannot be perceived by the blind, or by one ignorant of anatomy and optics. To feel the suitability of Christ as "The Truth," the mind must become aware of those great spiritual laws under which it is placed.

But while "The Truth" is thus perfectly adapted to our condition in this life, it is equally fitted for the soul in the life to come. "The Truth," which originates our spiritual life in time, will continue it

through eternity. Thus the Gospel doctrines never
die; while souls shall live in heaven, Truth shall
live in those souls. The redeemed will never forget
Gospel mysteries! When "made perfect," they
will remember their sinful state: when triumphant
over death, they will remember the grave: when
exulting in the strength of a heavenly life, they will
not forget the weaknesses of their earthly life.
What purpose will such memories answer? They
will ever keep before the multitudes of the saved
the glories of Him who is the great, pure, divine,
suitable, and everlasting "Truth!"

A Teacher from God.

John iii. 2.

Some teachers have been sent by evil spirits,*
others have been moved by ambition, by unholy
zeal,† by the energy of contradiction, or by the
mere love of dictation. Many have knowingly
taught a lie; others, being deceived, have uncon-
sciously proclaimed falsehood. A few have held
the poisoned cup of error to the lips of whole
nations, and stand out, with a terrible distinctness,
as the spiritual murderers of multitudes.

Truth, too, has had a long succession of teachers,
who have held up her heavenly light, even close to

* 1 Kings xxii. 22.   † Matt. xxiii. 15.

the heathen altars. Thus two classes of teachers
have been endeavouring to win the world. Which
has gained the most followers? A very short survey
supplies the answer; falsehood seems triumphant.
How is this? Is it because the teachers of truth
are but feeble expounders of glorious doctrines,
far above their grasp? Has no Divine teacher ever
yet appeared to uphold, by his sovereign authority,
the words of truth? Suppose, for a moment, that
we were compelled to answer thus:—"Truth has
had no preacher from the heavenly world; she must
rely for victory on human eloquence, learning, or
power." How deeply would all earnest hearts feel
a want; how hopeless would the great spiritual
struggle seem! The aspect of the whole case is
changed when, looking up to the Lord Jesus, we
can say, "Thou art a Teacher come from God."
Such an Instructor will give *sufficient* truth, and
His words must infallibly prevail over every form
of falsehood.

This Teacher from God might have given most
precious truths to the world, without even con-
descending to appear amongst men. Inspired
prophets and miraculously endowed seers could
have transmitted His lessons to mankind. By
these human agéncies the first ages of the world
were taught; but the time came when the Head
Teacher uttered, in His own person, the grand
words of Divine wisdom. He spoke in no academic
garden, in no philosophic porch, where the intellectual and the mighty only could have listened.

This greatest of all instructors spoke of heavenly
mysteries to fishermen by the side of the Galilæan
lake, to the unlettered Jewish peasants on the hill-
sides of Palestine, to the fallen and the outcasts in
the streets of Jerusalem. He knew all the deep
things of the universe, and could have revealed more
than reason shall ever discover. Some minds may
feel surprised that the Lord's teaching did not
unlock the mysteries of Nature, or settle at once
the problems of ages. But, in the fulness of His
love and pity, He saw that man needed spiritual
wisdom rather than science, and regeneration rather
than philosophy. When we remember, that in Him
were "all the treasures of wisdom and knowledge,"*
we are amazed at the beautiful condescension of
His lessons, and their exact adaptation to the
ignorance, weakness, and prejudice of man.

Yet how *original,* if such a word be here allowable,
was this Great Teacher. His wonderful parables, in
which the whole spiritual life of man is painted; the
familiar illustrations, carrying grand truths home to
the heart; the singular and overwhelming answers
to bitter questioners; and the comprehensive beauty
of His exhortations,—lead us to exclaim, with the
Jewish officers, "Never man spake like this man."†
The teaching of our Lord stands majestically alone,
without a parallel. Some highly-lauded qualities
are never mentioned by Him. The dazzling splendour of the heroic character, the majesty of intellect,
or the grandeur of genius, are passed without a

* Col. ii, 3. † John vii. 46.

notice! All His commendations are reserved for meekness, a forgiving spirit, a repentant heart, prayer, and trust in God. Such teaching would have amazed the great men of Pagan Rome, and have mightily perplexed the keen wits of Athens! Yet how completely fitted to transform earth into heaven!

The *authority* of His teaching is as remarkable as its originality. He builds nothing on human creeds, human systems, or human prejudice; relies on no great Rabbin, cites no famous author; but praises, condemns, commands, and teaches, as "One having authority."* As the Lord taught then, so He teaches now, by the silent yet mighty operations of the Holy Spirit. Well is it for churches, nations, and individual Christians to bear in mind the nearness of this Teacher.

If this truth be forgotten, all will go miserably wrong. The Bible itself, without the presence of Christ, will be a dead letter, yielding, perhaps, matter for endless controversy, but bringing no power into the heart. Magnificent churches and solemn services, without the Great Teacher's presence, may cherish a sentimental pietism, but will never become means of grace to the soul. Creeds, theological systems, religious services, spiritual organizations, and sacraments, can only have life in them, just in proportion as we can look up to Jesus, with the heartfelt acknowledgment, "Thou art a Teacher come from God."

* Matt. vii. 29.

THE TRUE LIGHT.

John i. 9.

False lights are numerous; their fatal and mis-
leading gleams have fallen upon every age and all
lands. Some burn on the high places of the earth,
and attract the eyes of millions. Mahommedism
holds up its torch, and bids 100,000,000 follow,
and Buddhism sheds its baleful radiance over
300,000,000 of human souls! Does it not seem as
if a host of evil spirits were holding out false lights,
in all directions, to lure the voyager to the rocks
and the quicksands? If we glance over the earth,
we mark with surprise the many flickering lights
rising from the moral waste. Not one of these
lights ever led a wanderer to the right path, yet
the thoughtless human traveller still trusts them.
The moment a new meteor rises, the benighted
wayfarers rush towards the treacherous gleam, and
are lost in the quicksands! Such is the scene which
meets our view, even in the nineteenth century!

But all this time there is a "True Light" shining!
It came not from the earth, for earth is not the
native home of light; but from the highest heavens,
where all is pure, bright, and true. Do we, do
churches, do nations really believe that one "True
Light" has been given to the earth? It is not a

speculative question; not a matter of mere probability; but a grand fact;—the "True Light" is amongst us! It discloses to us the nature of our life on earth, as a period of spiritual conflict, a time of grace, a day of salvation. It warns of the array of evil spirits conspiring against man, and points out the necessity and nearness of the Holy Spirit's help. This Light shines even beyond the present life, teaching our faith to realize the holy rest, to which regenerate and believing souls shall be admitted when called away from the body. It conducts our thoughts to the Resurrection, giving a sure promise of complete victory over the grave.

But how do we *know* the Light is indeed "True?" Try it; put this "Light" to the test of experience; shape your course by its guidance; and then say whether it has led you in a safe path or not. Surely this is the most decisive argument, and all may use this test. This "Light" was intended to be the guide of man's life; then try its fitness for this purpose. You may have little of reasoning skill; you may be unable to grasp all the details of a deep and wide argument; but you can, by the aid of offered grace, take the "True Light" for your guidance.

Many startling disclosures will be made "at the time of the end;"* but that period of searching will not find one soul, one church, or one nation which the "True Light" has failed to lead securely to the end. But this Divine Light must be followed

* Dan. xii. 4.

honestly and exclusively. If we walk by the "True Light" one day, and on the next substitute an earthly torch for the heavenly sun, we shall spend life in vexation or delusion. How many, both individuals and communities, are thus walking, partly right and partly wrong; striving to bind together heavenly truth and earthly fiction; conscious of the gloom, but not solely trusting the "True Light;" feeling that the sun has risen, yet walking by the glow worm's glimmer!

See what beams of brightness are shed on the path of life; rays of glory stream from the Mediatorial Throne; they are reflected from the Cross, and fall with a beautiful and hallowing clearness on every pilgrim's track! Let us, then, hear the voice from heaven, "Arise, shine! for thy Light is come, and the glory of the Lord is risen upon thee!"*

The Light of The World.

John viii. 12.

"Light, more Light," were the dying words of a famous poet,† and such language expresses the feeling of the whole human race. "I have met with no serious person," says Paley, "who thinks that, even under the Christian revelation, we have

---

* Isa. lx. 1.   † Göthe.

too much light." Certainly not ; for even the rays
of the Sun of Righteousness fall upon a dense and
murky atmosphere of sin.

The " Light of the World " is a grand title ; and
round Him who claims it the brightest hopes of
mankind must gather. How many lights, which
once glimmered for awhile, have been extinguished
for ever. Men have a faint recollection of certain
meteors which flashed for a moment across the deep
gloom, and were then lost in the darkness. Ancient
times tell, in mournful histories, of these lost lights ;
and there are men who, even now, are looking
towards the dark horizon for the rising of an expected star. Mourn no longer over the perished
luminaries of the past ; look not, with almost
hopeless gaze, for the first rays of some future
dawn. "The Light of the World" has already
come ; the sun is shining on high. Look no more
into the caves of earth for some torch, kindled by
human hands ; look *upwards*, there behold a Light
sufficient to guide all souls. He has not come to
illumine one privileged race, or one honoured nation
only ; but to fill the whole earth with His glory : He
alone is " The Light of the *World*." Some lights
may have been fitted for Egypt, some for Greece,
and others for Rome, but the Divine radiance of the
Sun of Righteousness breaks through all geogra-
phical limits. Its beams are as suited to the hut of
the Esquimaux, as to the home of the philosopher.

To whatever height of civilization mankind may
attain, they will ever need "The Light of the

World " to shed a hallowing splendour over intellectual riches. There is a kind of illumination which, like the ever-burning lamps in idol temples, guides the soul to sin. " The Light of men "* is essentially hallowing ; and, without it, the most magnificent temple of human genius will be desecrated. Therefore it happens, that no system of state-craft, no laws constructed by the wisdom of ages, will keep or make society pure, unless " The Light of the World " be ever shining there. This result is to be expected; for how could Christ be rightly called the World's Light, if any nation or kingdom could reach true happiness without Him ? The one " Light" for the world, being adapted to all countries and all times, will for ever remain the only source of illumination for the human race. Earth may grow old, the ruins of once mighty empires may tell of vanished terrestrial glory ; but high above all the swellings of Time's troubled sea, like a lighthouse on a storm-beaten rock, " The Light of the World " will stand the hope of all people.

A man cannot see the sun even when it is shining in mid-day splendour, if he obstinately fix his eyes on the ground, or dwell in the depths of a dark cavern. All the rich beauty of summer brightness may be close to that man and he know it not. Has " The Light of the World " shone into our hearts, revealing the poverty of the creature, and the riches of glory in Christ Jesus ? then no path of life can be dark, and even death's valley shall be bright.

* John i. 4.

THE BRIGHT AND THE MORNING STAR.

Rev xxii. 16.

The evening star suggests thoughts of subsiding energy; while the deepening gloom and the silent approach of darkness seem like a death spreading over nature.   Such is the hour when the poet might be led to compose " An Elegy in a country church-yard," the growing stillness of the landscape naturally suggesting thoughts of the rest to which all men are approaching.

Far different are the thoughts which arise in the heart at the sight of the clear and brilliant " Morning Star."   Then we know that the day is coming, and all things are awaking to receive the influence of the pure and stimulating light.

The " Morning Star," therefore, represents the Lord as the great preparer of mankind for the coming of that brighter day when the full sunlight of the heavenly glory shall illumine every redeemed spirit.   We see not yet the brightness of the holy land ; for the present is the hour of growing, but not of perfect, light.   " Life and immortality " are indeed made known by our Teacher ; but we have not the full manifestation ; all men see as yet " through a glass darkly."   The light is freely given, but it is that of " The Morning Star"; the full sun is however

G

coming, the clouds are breaking, and all creation is waiting for the beauty of the day-spring.*

Though we have not on earth all the promised light, though "we know in part," yet the rays which reach us are all pure; they come from heaven, not from the fires of earth; the "Morning Star" gives out nothing but a Divine radiance. As every star would appear a sun could we approach sufficiently near, so the "Morning Star" will be found to be the Sun of Righteousness. From this distant earth we look, by the aid of a far-reaching and penetrating faith, into the unseen world, and feel assured that Jesus, who veils His glory, now appearing as the "Morning Star," will one day permit us to "see Him as He is."†

This more distinct revelation of His brightness is promised by the Saviour to all who conquer in His name. "I will give him the Morning Star,"‡ are the emphatic and remarkable words spoken to those who are faithfully walking by the light already given. They who shall be blessed with such an illumination, will indeed be fitly called "saints in light."§

The future Messiah was announced by Balaam to the heathen of his own age, in the remarkable words, "There shall come a Star out of Jacob."‖ This man of vacillating heart took no comfort from his own glowing prophecy. "I shall behold Him,

* Rom. viii. 22, 23.   † 1 John iii. 2.   ‡ Rev. ii. 28.   § Col. i. 12.
‖ Numb. xxiv. 17. This passage was regarded by Onkelos, a famous and ancient Rabbi, as a prediction of the Messiah.

but not nigh," were the mournful words uttered by that singular prophet. "The vision of the Almighty" overcame him, and the seer, "having his eyes open," was compelled to predict the rising of the " Star."

Strange does it seem, that the prophet who announced to the ancient Church the coming Star, who beheld from the mount of prophecy the triumph of the Messiah's kingdom, should in sullen obduracy of heart turn from the Divine " Star " to a false worship. Notwithstanding the abundance of his revelations, an ominous gloom hangs over his name whenever mentioned.* The " Morning Star" shines before many now as clearly as it appeared in vision to Balaam ; but they turn from the pure beams of heaven, and try to find the path of life by the aid of earth's dim lanterns.

As a " Star," Christ was foretold to Israel in the wilderness, and it was " His Star in the East "† which led the " wise men " from distant regions to Jerusalem, at the very time the unconscious world had just received its Lord. When the light of the " Morning Star" enters the hearts of men, it produces a threefold effect. Such become, in the highest sense, " wise men," receiving that discernment of heart by which they estimate rightly things temporal and things eternal. If those who love wisdom are truly called philosophers, surely they who receive the " wisdom of God " are students of the highest philosophy.

All who are enlightened by the beams of the

* 2 Peter ii 15; Jude 11; Rev. ii. 14. † Matt. ii. 2.

G 2

soul's "Morning Star," will leave their native
country of ignorance, superstition, or formalism,
that they may come near to the Great Light-giver.
They become spiritual pilgrims and are always safely
guided, for the Star goes "before them."

And what is the result of this enlightenment?
They rejoice, they worship, and present the gifts
most acceptable to the Lord; themselves just as
they are, absolutely and without conditions. It
matters not to them where Christ is found; it may
be in a manger—they worship Him there nevertheless.

The light of a star is not affected by that on which
it falls; it is equally pure, whether shining on a stagnant
pool, or on a crystal fountain. In like manner
the rays of "the Morning Star" come with the same
purifying power into the gloomiest dens of human sin
and misery as into hearts long made holy by the
power of grace. Let it penetrate through dungeon
bars into felons' cells, the ray will be hallowing there.
As the murkiness of our atmosphere affects not the
stars, so all the corruptions of the world and the
Church never really affect the unchanging Gospel of
Christ. Men may cover their eyes with many veils
of brilliant colours, and suppose the rays of "the
Morning Star" have changed. To attack the Gospel
because men have united their Christianity to superstition,
is as unreasonable as to suppose the stars
extinguished when our eyes are covered.

Let the Christian remember that his whole life,
since conversion to God, is but a morning;—"the

night is far spent, the day is at hand,"*—and the clear shining of "the Morning Star" reminds us of that dawn which brings on the day of Eternity. It is the time of preparation; a higher life is at hand; but only those who reverently use the light of "the Morning Star," will be fitted for the land where there is no night.

* Rom. xiii. 12.

———◆———

Titles of our Lord

THE HOLY AND ALL-SUFFICIENT SACRIFICE.

———◆———

THE HOLY ONE OF GOD.
THE LAMB OF GOD.
THE PASSOVER.
THE HIGH PRIEST.
THE PROPITIATION.
THE ONE MEDIATOR.
OUR PEACE.

THESE seven titles bring the Saviour before us as The Spotless Sacrifice, who has procured for His Church an everlasting peace. *The Holy One of God* reminds us of Him who was "without sin," and therefore fitted to be a perfect oblation. *The Lamb of God* proclaims the Lord as the Father's appointed and accepted offering for man : and the appropriate words, *Our Passover*, shew the security of those upon whom His precious blood has been sprinkled. As *High Priest* we see Him entering the mysterious Holy of Holies once for all. *The Propitiation* sets Him forth as the reconciler of the world. As *The One Mediator* He stands ready to confer upon the Church all the benefits of His wondrous suffering ; and as *Our Peace* He will ere long bring in the grand Millenium, for which the whole creation is waiting.

THE HOLY ONE OF GOD.

Mark i. 24.

Great is the difference between holy ones and *The* Holy One. The pure spirits who have kept their " first estate," the souls who have passed into the heavenly resting places, and all the regenerated on earth, are among the former. He who is " the Image of the invisible God," bears the peculiar title of The Holy One. All creature holiness, whether in angels or men, is *received ;* the holiness of the Lord is inherent. The goodness of redeemed men has a beginning, a time from which it dates; the Holy One has been such from eternity.

What shall we copy ? Whom shall we strive to imitate ? Such inquiries meet with various answers.

One bids us walk in the track of the great men of
olden times, and thus make our lives sublime.
Another proposes for our admiration devoted Christians who have glorified the Saviour on the earth.
Such examples are not to be neglected ; "whatsoever
things are lovely "* are to be sought, and we are
earnestly to follow the footsteps of those who now
" inherit the promises."† But our true exemplar is
the Holy One of God. He is the ever-shining Sun
in morals ; the only perfect pattern of a holy life.
In the best of human models we see a dark edge
round the brightest virtues, and seductive errors are
mingled with excellencies.

But in the Holy One of God all is the unbroken
harmony of goodness. " Follow thou Me "‡ is
therefore the heavenly rule for those who seek an
unerring guide, a perfect pattern. The " Imitation
of Christ " is but another expression for a truly
Christian life.

Does any one say such an exemplar is far too high
for weak, ignorant, and tempted man. Reflect a
moment on the unbelief, the infidelity, implied in
such a feeling. Did Christ design His life for "an
example "?§ Is it not a grand, an amazing truth,
that Christ is " our life "‖ now, and that grace
sufficient for our work is promised ? The objection
might be valid in the mouth of an unbeliever, who
denies the doctrine of Divine influence, or rejects
the help of God. Certainly none can imitate the

* Phil. iv. 8.   † Heb. vi. 12.   ‡ John xxi. 22.   § 1 Peter ii. 21.
‖ Col. iii. 4.

life of the Holy One unless power from above be given. But herein is one proof of the Gospel suitability to man, that it offers strength for duties enjoined.

The holiness of Jesus is peculiarly attractive, being marked by all that is loving, truthful, and Godlike. It was exhibited in His character when young, shone brightly in His works of love and pity, characterized Him in poverty, marked Him among the rich, was displayed in His wondrous teaching, and manifested a Divine beauty amid the insults and the humiliation of His death. He, who thus showed Himself the Holy One, is now in the heavens, having by His memorable prayer, " Sanctify them through thy truth,"* secured perfect and everlasting holiness for all who commit themselves to His keeping.

THE LAMB OF GOD.

John i. 29.

The idea of a sacrifice for sin was deeply implanted in the heart of man. In the earliest ages, among the rudest and most uncivilized tribes, we see conscience-stricken men sacrificing selected victims. The notion, too, of a human sacrifice, was widely spread. The Grecian chief, Agamemnon, offended the goddess of his people, and his daughter was

* John xvii. 17.

demanded as a victim. "Shall I give my first-born
for my transgression ?"* was a question which the
perplexed conscience of the heathen might well
suggest.

This almost universal feeling sprang from no
delusion; human sin was no fiction; and the idea of
an atonement met the craving of the guilty soul.

To preserve this truth from corruption, and to
hold it up before the nations, was one object of the
Mosaic dispensation; which exhibited, in all its
peculiar ceremonies, the doctrine of an atonement.
The daily sacrifice proclaimed twice every day to the
Jew the coming of the great propitiation. Every
true Israelite must have felt, when contemplating the
incessant round of victims, that these were but
figures " for the time then present."†

At length, in " the fulness of time," the types
were all satisfied, and the grand words were first
heard, " Behold the Lamb of God." This was the
most significant sentence ever heard by men. But
its utterance was unattended by any display of pomp
or power. A bold, simple, and earnest teacher proclaimed it, the fisherman and the rustic heard it, and
two inquiring Jews sought further information.‡
That day was nevertheless one of the critical days
of earth; one of the ever-memorable times in the
imperishable records of the Divine dealings with
man. All typical victims, all typical altars, had
accomplished their work; for the glorious anti-type
had come.

* Micah vi. 7.   † Heb. ix. 9.   ‡ John i. 37.

How full of meaning is this short title, " The Lamb of God." Men had provided the typical lambs, but this wondrous sacrifice descended from heaven, taking into mysterious union with Himself a miraculously prepared body.* The earth was the altar to be hallowed by that most sacred blood, but God Himself provided the priceless offering.

Even " before the foundation of the world " this " Lamb of God " was ordained ;† the vast and wondrous plan of our redemption having been prepared long before sin appeared on the earth. The unbelieving Jews, or the Roman soldiers who witnessed the Crucifixion, may have traced it to the hatred of the priests or the fury of the people. Perhaps not one of the spectators of that amazing sacrifice knew that then and there the eternal counsels were being accomplished.

The typical lambs were to be without blemish, and " The Lamb of God " was a perfect sacrifice.‡ One offering sufficed for all sin, for all mankind, and for all the ages of time. Being thus perfect it freed the dying thief from every stain of guilt ; he needed no time for prayers, for works of faith or holy living ; the sacrifice could have saved in one moment a whole world of such repenting sinners.

The typical lambs were taken from a race of inferior creatures ;—" The Lamb of God " bore a sinless *humanity*. The body nailed to the Cross, pierced by the Roman spear, and laid in the Jewish grave, was human. The soul which was " exceeding

* John i. 14 ; Luke i. 35 ; Heb. x. 5.   † 1 Peter i. 20.   ‡ Heb. x. 14.

sorrowful,"* which "was in all points tempted like
as we are,"† was, in all its faculties, a pure and
perfect human soul.   Thus the punishment for man's
sin was suffered by man's nature.   The fallen angels
can therefore never say that human sin has been
unpunished.

"The Lamb of God" was a *Divine* sacrifice.‡
The union of God and man in one Christ compels us
to believe, that in the atoning death on Calvary, the
Divine nature was co-operating with the human, in
the grand mystery of redemption.   The efficacy,
therefore, of "the precious blood of Christ,"§ is far
beyond the power of created minds to estimate.

"The Lamb of God" was an *exclusive* sacrifice.||
It stands alone, the only means of salvation.   All
the prayers of the Church from the beginning of
time, all the sufferings of martyrs, all the holy works
of self-denying saints, are utterly worthless as *saving*
powers.   The Cross alone opens heaven; salvation
is purchased, but the only price is the blood of
Christ.

"The Lamb of God" was a *universal* sacrifice.¶
No imagination has, probably, ever yet conceived
the vastness of the blessings obtained by the atoning
death of Christ.   They extend over all ages—from
the beginning to the end of time; comprehending,
doubtless, all unsinning infants, and countless
multitudes in many lands.   These blessings reach
far beyond this world: the joys of heaven continued

* Mark xiv. 34. ‡ Acts. xx. 28. || Acts iv. 12.
† Heb. iv. 15.   § 1 Peter i. 19.   ¶ 1 John ii. 2.

through eternity, and enjoyed by innumerable souls, are the direct results of this universal sacrifice. "The Lamb of God" is the great *reconciler* of man to his Maker.* The war between earth and heaven must ever be an awful mystery; "the origin of evil" a deep perplexity; but in the work finished on the Cross, God was "in Christ reconciling the world unto Himself."† The world shall no longer be alien, but will ere long be united in full harmony to the great family of God.

Let each Christian reflect that this Divine, human, perfect, exclusive, universal, and reconciling sacrifice, was offered and accepted for him. Let faith gaze on this "Lamb of God," until all guilt is felt to be removed; until love shall constrain the heart to live for Him who died; until hope shall rise on seraph-like wing, and the redeemed soul, in adoring surrender, consecrate every power to the service of the "Lamb that was slain."‡

The Passover.

1 Cor. v. 7.

The celebration of the Passover in the old times, before the sceptre departed from Judah, must have been a period of great national exultation. The memory of the deliverance from Egypt, the marvel

---

* Col. i. 20.   † 2 Cor. v. 19.   ‡ Rev. v. 12.

wrought on the shores of the Red Sea, the miracles
of the desert, and the long ages of mercy and of
judgment, by which the nation had been disciplined,
would then deeply touch the heart of the religious
Jew. The commemorative sacrifice drew the Israelite
from the most remote regions, and round the paschal
lamb were gathered the sons of Abraham from the
Parthian deserts, and the shores of Africa. The
Jewish child then often received the first vivid impression of his nation's wondrous history, and many
a hoary-headed father of Israel shed tears of joy as
he gazed on the three millions of worshippers, pouring through the streets of Jerusalem.*

But the Jew who understood the significance of
the paschal sacrifice, and had comprehended the
predictions of the prophets, must have often asked,
" when will this great typical ceremony be accomplished;" when will the great Passover appear?—
At last there came a day most awful for Jerusalem,
never to be forgotten by men or angels, when the
rejected Messiah was led by the prejudiced, excited
multitude to the cross. That crowd had joined, a
few hours before, in celebrating the very sacrifice
which typified "The Lamb of God," the one perfect
oblation was offered in their presence, but they knew
it not. A strange, an awful darkness gathered over
the city, emblematical of the spiritual night prevail-
ing there; and amidst the deep gloom an earthquake

* Josephus gives, as the lowest possible number on one occasion,
two millions seven hundred thousand and two hundred. (Jewish War,
Book, vi. 9.)

spoke, as if to startle into life the dying conscience of the people. In the midst of these signs "Our Passover" was sacrificed, once for all people, once for all ages. The Jewish historian tells that, at one paschal feast, two hundred and fifty-six thousand and five hundred lambs were slain. These, being types only, were many; the antitype "Our Passover," was sufficient in Himself alone.

The word "our" indicates one peculiar glory of the Lord's sacrifice. The Jew might exult in the exclusiveness of his Passover; the Gospel salvation came without regard to nationalities, but the term "our" suggests another thought. Have we made this sacrifice "Our Passover," by a glad acceptance, by a grateful partaking? The Israelite who refused to join in the paschal solemnity, was to be cut off from the commonwealth of Israel;* and in vain is a Christian name, an orthodox creed, and an outward participation in holy services, if "Our Passover" be in reality rejected by the heart.

The Mosaic rite was celebrated, not by solitary worshippers, isolated from their brethren, but in united companies, not less than ten to each lamb. And one great object of the Saviour's perfect sacrifice is to unite regenerated men in holy communities, joining in works of faith and hymns of praise. The cross is the uniter of hearts, and from this will surely follow a co-operation of hands. Never did Israel seem so completely united as when celebrating her Passover; never are Christians so much one body

* Num. ix. 13.

as when living in daily contemplation of the work
finished on Calvary. Is it not the want of this
heart religion which now separates churches and
individuals; spreading far and wide that schism of
souls, which has been so long the bane of the church?

"Our Passover" is ever present; thus exhibiting
a marked contrast to the ancient rite, which was
witnessed but once a year. Christians cannot live
upon mere memories; the soul requires constant
accessions of strength; and this the Lord imparts to
the waiting, believing multitudes, who in all lands
celebrate the grand feast of love and redemption.

The typical Passover reminded the Israelite of
deliverance, both from Pharaoh's tyranny and the
angel's fatal stroke. But "Our Passover" has
secured us from the despotism of the world, the flesh,
and the devil. These three tyrannies have ruled over
mighty kingdoms, and have crushed into the dust of
an abject slavery the greatest conquerors. But such
fearful powers of evil cannot take possession of the
home on which the blood of the great sacrifice has
been sprinkled. The extent of our deliverance is
not yet fully known. The experience of life but
partly reveals it; the hour of death will still further
declare its nature; but the revelations of the future
state, and the solemnities of the judgment will shew
its completeness.

It might have seemed strange to many a Hebrew,
that the preservation of the people should depend
on the shedding of blood. "Why can we not be
rescued," some might have suggested, "by the

divine mercy alone, without the slaughter of so many innocent victims, and such numerous sprinklings of blood?" To such inquiries no reply would have been given; except the alternative,—obey or perish. In vain do men ask now "why was the sacrifice of the cross necessary?" The only answer comes with a solemn distinctness, "without shedding of blood, is no remission."* The full reasons for the wondrous mystery may be given in the future world; the great law of salvation is now clear enough, "believe on the Lord Jesus Christ, and thou shalt be saved."† He who will not receive the fact, unless the mystery be also made clear, must be left to perish.

The Israelites partook of the paschal lamb dressed as travellers for an immediate journey; and all who can truly call Christ Jesus " Our Passover," must also be ready to go forth, not only as pilgrims on the earth,‡ but as trained runners of a most arduous race.§ The road may cross deserts, and will certainly descend into the valley of death, yet shall they enter into the beautiful land, and find everlasting rest in the city of their God.

The Passover, though a feast, was accompanied by memorials of sorrow. The lamb was eaten with " bitter herbs;" no thoughtful Israelite could then forget the Egyptian bondage; none could ignore national and personal sins, or be filled with vain glory in the presence of such suggestive symbols. In like manner, all who "keep the feast" of the

---

* Heb. ix. 22.   † Acts xvi. 31.   ‡ Heb. xi. 13.   § Heb. xii. 1.

H

Gospel Passover, know the "godly sorrow" which worketh repentance to salvation,* and unite the solemn remembrance of sin with hymns of thanksgiving. The deepest humiliation is often close to the holiest joy.

From the celebration of the first Passover, the Jews dated the commencement of their national life; and from the moment when Christ is received into the heart, as the only purifier of the conscience,† we trace the life of each regenerated spirit. This is the true chronology of the Christian; his great epochs begin with the work of the Saviour for him and in him. Let us therefore rejoice; we have an everlasting festival, which no change of time, no long succession of ages, will render obsolete. Jerusalem may never again witness the old paschal solemnities; but until time shall cease the church of God will have her festal joys, and when "time shall be no longer," the children of the heavenly King will celebrate the redeeming sacrifice of Him who is "Our Passover."

The High Priest.

Heb. ii. 17; iii. 1; iv. 15; v. 5, 10.

The priesthood met the eye of the Jew in all parts of the old Temple service. In prayer and praise, in fast and festival; in the hour of national sorrow and

---

* 2 Cor. vii. 10.   † Heb. ix. 14.

in the day of high triumph, the priest was ever present. In a far higher sense such is the fact still.

The Church collectively, each Christian individually, sees and feels, at every step of spiritual progress, the influence of our Great "High Priest." The idea of a sacrifice is as present to the mind of a believer in Christ, as it was to the Israelite of old. In this great principle the two dispensations are in perfect harmony.

Let us contemplate some particulars in the character and work of the Christian's "High Priest."

Under the law the priest and the sacrifice were distinct; the Gospel brings before us a High Priest who offers up Himself. No other victim could be found sufficiently precious in earth or heaven; the High Priest of the world presented Himself, and became the sacrifice. The priests of the old dispensation were human and sinful; the Sacrificer under the Gospel was man, but sinless; thus exhibiting the only instance of a priest who needed no sacrifice for himself. The sons of Aaron, however magnificent their ceremonial, could claim no higher nature than that of Adam; our "High Priest" was not only "with God," but "was God."*

Thus earth and heaven beheld the amazing union of sinlessness, humanity, and Divinity in this "High Priest." Such a sacrifice and such an offering could be required but once. The typical victims were indeed slain daily, for they were but signs pointing to Him who "should come";† but the full, perfect,

* John i. 1.   † Luke vii. 19.

H 2

and sufficient oblation" presented by our "High Priest," can never be repeated. As "by one offering He hath perfected for ever them that are sanctified,"* the merits of that precious sacrifice will avail for every age of the world's history, for every nation of the human race.

The Jew, in ancient times, saw with each returning year a new day of atonement; the earth has witnessed but one day of Calvary, but one entry of the Great "High Priest" into that invisible Holy of Holies, which is for a time hidden by a veil, impenetrable, save to a spiritual vision.   Jesus was seen entering;† He is now within the sanctuary, acting as our sacrificial Mediator; He will reappear to utter that glorious benediction, "Come ye blessed of My Father";‡ which shall close all the services of time.

Let us often, by faith, follow Him into the heavenly place,§ where the hourly and daily intercession is made by the Redeemer for the redeemed.

The first Jewish high priest was anointed by Moses with a special perfume, appropriated to the temple and the priests only;‖ but the Son of God was chosen as our first, only, and everlasting "High Priest," before the foundation of the world,¶ by the eternal Father.   Nor was a visible consecration of a most solemn and significant kind wanting.   The heavens were strangely opened, men saw a suggestive symbol of the Holy Ghost resting on the head of the Lord at this anointing, while mysterious words

* Heb. x. 14.   † Acts i. 9.   ‡ Matt. xxv. 34.
§ Heb. vi. 19.   ‖ Ex xxx. 33.   ¶ 1 Peter i. 20.

marked out the true "High Priest" of men.* One
such anointing suffices for ever; the priesthood of
Jesus knows no change, no succession; as He is our
first "High Priest," so is He the last.

His office is "for ever."† In this respect the
Jewish priesthood, with all its changes and abrupt
termination, was but a feeble type of our Redeemer.
No earthly figures can fully represent heavenly mysteries. Faith, hope, and love, under the abiding
influence of the Divine Teacher, may read the truths
of eternity in the alphabets of time; but our clearest
insight is seeing "through a glass darkly."‡

It is therefore no marvel that a changeable priesthood should be an imperfect type of that which is
everlasting; of which the former was but "a figure
for the time then present."§ The Apostle, therefore, when treating of the never-ending priesthood
of the Lord, selects that mysterious friend of
Abraham, the ancient patriarch, who united in
himself the dignities of "King of Salem" and
"Priest of the Most High God," as a more exact
type of Christ, who is "made a High Priest for ever
after the order of Melchisedec."‖ Even the Jewish
Church of old times was directed to see in this
remarkable character the type of a higher priesthood
than that of Aaron.

In that grand Old Testament revelation, given in
the 110th Psalm, the Son is addressed as "a priest
for ever after the order of Melchisedec." This

* Luke iii. 21, 22. † Heb. vi. 20. ‡ 1 Cor. xiii. 12.
§ Heb. ix. 9. ‖ Heb. vi. 20.

singular and " great " man comes nearest of all the
Old Testament worthies to a perfect type of our
" High Priest." He who bore the titles, " King of
Righteousness," and " King of Peace," who is
described as having " neither beginning of days, nor
end of life," and abiding " a priest continually,"*
may well be set before us as a " similitude " of our
heavenly High Priest.

As the victorious Abraham made his rich offering
to Melchisedec the type, so will the whole redeemed
Church of God for ever present all her highest
services to the Father, through Him who is the
" High Priest over the house of God."†

The sympathy, faithfulness, mercy, and greatness
of our Divine Priest should lead us to commit with
most absolute confidence, to His loving keeping,
our temporal and eternal state ! His sympathy must
be perfect, for it is the sympathy of God, and of
Him who has mingled with men, has tasted suffering,
and borne temptation. Nothing is too small for the
pity of the exalted High Priest. Entrust, then,
everything to the all-loving, all-wise, all-merciful,
who walks where we walk, goes where we go, and is
ever speaking to listening ears, the words of guidance,
love and safety.

Let us never forget that we, if resting on Him,
are invested by our great Master with a priestly
character. He has made us " priests unto God."‡

Our life is therefore consecrated in Him, to a
hallowed and everlasting service, which, beginning on

* Heb. vii. 2, 3.   † Heb. x. 21.   ‡ Rev. i. 6.

the earth, and continuing by His loving help through
all changes of our mortal state, shall be perpe-
tuated in the holy mansions of the Father. In the
meantime, all necessary grace is infallibly secured
for us. Temptations may enter the heart, for evil
angels are close to us; faith may sometimes fail in
keenness of spiritual sight, for the earthly horizon is
often dark; but hold fast this great truth, that our
cause has been undertaken, our wants weighed, our
dangers understood, and our whole history is known
by Him, who "having obtained eternal redemption
for us," is now ever acting as our one, only, loving,
merciful, and faithful " High Priest."

THE PROPITIATION.

Rom. iii. 25 ; 1 John ii. 2 ; iv. 10.

Is God angry with me ? has often been the
inquiry of the conscience-stricken heart. The
solemn answer has been given in the affirmative.
Various then have been the devices by which the
affrighted soul has sought to appease its Maker.
Horrid rites were performed in the darkness of
groves, and beneath the thick gloom of night.
Human blood stained many an ancient altar, and
terrified men devoted infants to Moloch. This
deeply-seated feeling of the heart was no delusion.
The wild superstitions of the heathen pointed to an
awful reality, a fearful alienation between the Creator

and the creature. Can this terrible hostility be terminated ? The sacrifices on Druidical, Grecian, or Roman altars, seemed to hint of the possibility of appeasing the great, though insulted, Father of all. But no reliable promise was given, to which the heart could cling ; and even untutored reason must have whispered how impossible it was "that the blood of bulls and of goats should take away sin."* The anxious mind looked in vain for a true "propitiation." The semblance was indeed everywhere, the reality nowhere.

How remarkably was the trembling uncertainty of the heart shewn in the last hours of that famous Athenian,† who is often singled out as the type of the highest Pagan excellence. Just before his death, this greatest philosopher of the ancient world ordered a victim to be sacrificed to one of the Greek divinities. He dared not enter the unknown home of spirits, without making an attempt to propitiate one at least of his country's gods.

Many a rich spiritual blessing entitles the religion of Jesus to be called the Gospel, or Good Word, and the announcement of an all-sufficient "propitiation" stands in the front of these heavenly gifts. Here we find in reality, what every altar, every victim, every priest of the Pagan world was but a semblance. Sin may have attached to it a train of consequences too long and too fearful for any human mind to grasp, and infinite justice may be an attribute too awful for our contemplation ; but a divinely

* Heb. x. 4.   † Socrates, put to death 399 B.C.

provided "propitiation" enables us to look, not only with calmness, but with joy on God in Christ. The procurer of an everlasting reconciliation is "set forth"* by the Father for our acceptance ; the offended Law-giver has prepared the appeasing gift.

The word rendered "propitiation"† in Rom. iii. 25, is translated "mercy-seat" in Heb. ix. 5, and we are thus reminded that as the mercy-seat completely covered the ark, containing the tables of the broken law, so Christ our "propitiation" hides and covers over for ever, the whole accumulation of sin. His righteousness as effectually veils our transgressions, as the golden cover of the ark concealed the stone tablets which spoke of condemnation. Had the golden lid been lifted, the terrors of Sinai might have been read within the ark ; and if the "propitiation" be removed there is no peace, though we may be visibly seated in the holy places of the Church.

The mercy-seat or propitiation, was close to the tables of the law ; and so our Redeemer does not appease justice by putting the law far away, but unites in beautiful harmony the mercy of the Father, with the truth of the everlasting testimonies. The "righteousness" of the Divine rule and the "peace" of the propitiation "have kissed each other."‡

The law in all its perfection, the whole and not a part, was covered by the mercy-seat ; and every soul who shall enter the "many mansions" of heaven, will not fear to look upon the fulness of the com-

* Rom. iii, 25.　　† 'Ιλαστήριον　　‡ Ps. lxxxv. 10.

mandment, though it be exceeding broad."* Christ
being made unto us "righteousness,"† the perfect
law may now ask of us a perfect righteousness, and
it is immediately presented, in our name, by the
" propitiation."

The pure gold of the mercy-seat, the symbolical
ark, and the tablets of the law, have long disap-
peared; being superfluous when the true "propitiation" came. Symbols pass away, but substance
remains; types vanish, but the anti-type stands.
The appeasing righteousness of the Lord shall never
be set aside; never become an institution of the
past. To the close of earthly history, its power
shall be felt; through all the ages of the life to come
its infinite efficacy will remain. The mercy-seat was
not placed in the court of the tabernacle, or in the
holy place, but in the Holy of Holies; and the far
extended results of the Gospel "propitiation"
cannot be completely apprehended on earth. When
we shall see "the King in His beauty," we may
comprehend His work in its glory.

The mysterious figures of the cherubim were
always contemplating the mercy-seat,‡ and this may
serve to remind us of the deep and adoring reverence
with which the angels "look into"§ the work of
redemption. It was a solemn, silent watch, those
cherubims kept from year to year above the mercy-
seat, the ark and the law. Heavenly and holy
watchers,‖ may be observing now the triumphs of

* Ps. cxix. 96.   † 1 Cor. i. 30.   ‡ Heb. ix. 5.
§ 1 Pet. i. 12.   ‖ Dan. iv. 13.

mercy and of judgment, and waiting for the day
when they shall be summoned to witness the completion of the Saviour's propitiatory work.

Do we earnestly desire to feel ourselves at "perfect
peace" with God, to receive deep into our hearts
the hallowing comfort which our blessed Lord
bestows, and to secure a quietude of spirit which
shall become deeper with each year of life, and
grow into a heavenly calm when death draws near?
Then let us ever be looking by faith on our one
perfect and everlasting "propitiation."

The One Mediator.

1 Tim. ii. 5.

The human heart craves for a Mediator, for some
Mighty One who should stand between fallen man
and his Maker. When conscious of guilt, but
ignorant of a Saviour, the soul endeavours, as did
Adam, to escape from the presence of a pure heart-
searching and omnipotent God. In his terror man
makes for himself altars, sacrifices, and priests to
whom he clings as mediators. Even the spirits of
departed men, the heroes of olden times, were fondly
regarded as mediatorial beings, more closely allied
with human wants than the pure creative spirit
could be. In the midst of all this groping in the
dark, do we not see the influence of a feeling which
the Gospel is fitted to meet?

But the Mediator which man needs must be exalted above the creature, and yet connected with the Creator; one having power with God, and yet sympathizing with man. One acquainted with the deep secrets of the eternal God, yet able to understand even the temptations of men.* Such, and far more than this in every possible degree of fitness, is " The One Mediator between God and men," revealed to us in the Gospel. We need no more shrink, sinners though we be, from approaching the Father of lights, because there is not " any daysman betwixt us."† The eternal Word, the well-beloved of the everlasting Father, " the Man Christ Jesus," has taken upon Himself the government of this world, until "the end" shall come ?‡ He is now among us, and in Him God is " reconciling the world unto Himself,"§ having sent into our very homes " the word of reconciliation.".

The world is therefore now placed under a wonderful and divinely appointed mediatorial system. The Father " hath put all things under " the Son,‖ who " must reign till He hath put all enemies under His feet." Such an amazing scheme probably marks the last age of human history, the final era of that long probation given to mankind.

Let us remember that our " One Mediator " has willingly passed through all those varieties of human life, by which He became " in all things " like unto men, sin excepted.¶ A great mystery is here,

* Heb. iv. 15.   ‡ 1 Cor. xv. 24.   ‖ 1 Cor. xv. 27.
† Job. ix. 33.   § 2 Cor. v. 19.   ¶ Heb. ii. 17.

into the depths of which no intellect can pierce, but
the simplest Christian may see and feel how wonderfully the Lord's life on earth fitted Him to be
" our Mediator." Such a high office requires the
closest knowledge of our weakness, wants, joys,
sorrows and temptations.

The Saviour knows them all ; whether they belong
to infancy, childhood, youth, or manhood. Old age,
as we may count it, He did not indeed reach ; but
that awful concentration of suffering, which marked
the last years of the Lord's sojourn among men,
brought with it an experience of sorrow, such as a
Methuselah could not have known.

If this perfect sympathy of Jesus, with all possible
conditions of a Christian's life, were more comprehended, more realized by us, He would be the *first*
to whom the troubled heart would betake itself.
" To which of the saints,"* or " angels,"† would the
wandering spirit have turned, had the " gentleness"‡
of the Lord, in dealing with sin-stricken hearts, been
fully apprehended. Strange that men should seek
help from departed souls, who, having sinned, need
a Mediator for themselves, and turn from Him in
whom are found all human and Divine perfections.
Had we seen Him at one of those moments when
His sympathies were made known by visible signs ;
when He took the little Jewish children in His arms ;§
when He rebuked the ambitious disputes of His disciples by seating a child close to Him,‖ or when the

* Job v. 1.   † Col. ii. 18   ‡ 2 Cor. x 1.
§ Mark x. 16.   ‖ Luke ix. 47.

sinless Redeemer wept at the tomb—then we should
have felt Him to be a friend for every emergency.
We should not have hesitated in bringing our
smallest troubles before Him. But the Lord has
not changed; and we may therefore feel assured
that He shews to all, who trust Him, the same
tender loving sympathy, which He manifested when
walking before men. If we do not realize that He
is, though invisible, among us still, protecting,
aiding, and guiding all His chosen ones, with a love
unutterable, we shall not be conscious of His mighty
workings as Mediator. It pleases the Redeemer,
for the present, to operate unseen, but faith is
called, not only to acknowledge, but to "rejoice
with joy unspeakable" in her unseen Lord.*   The
Mediator will indeed work close to us, though we
regard not; but how much of hallowing joy shall
we lose by our blindness. How deeply interested
are we in our Mediator's work. "All things work
together" under His direction; events in the extreme West, and changes in the utmost East, are
all tending to one result, "for good to them that
love God."†   Whenever, therefore, a believer in
Christ surveys the wide field of history, or hears of
vast changes in distant lands, or notes the ceaseless
ebb and flow of human things, he knows that all
this complex system of life is in the hands of his
Mediator, who has "power over all flesh."‡   Thus
the Saviour is "all and in all,"§ to every Christian.
Through the " One Mediator " come pardon, sanc-

* 1 Pet. i. 8.   † Rom. viii. 28.   ‡ John xvii. 2.   § Col. iii. 11.

tification, and all-sufficient grace, to each faithful
heart. By the "One Mediator," seated at the
Father's right hand,* and having the government
of the world "upon his shoulder,"† the kingdoms
of the earth shall be held, as with a bridle, until the
end come. Thus the One Mediator rules the world,
for our good, in the Father's name. But He is also
acting in our names in heaven ; for there He ever
presents that sacrifice of infinite value, before which
the accusations of hell are silent.

Under the first dispensation Moses discharged the
office of mediator for a short time, and for one small
people, by receiving the law for them, praying for
the rebellious nation, pointing to the remedy for
their diseases, and guiding them as the messenger
of God. But how much "more excellent "‡ is the
mediation of the Lord Jesus, being for all ages, all
nations, and communicating everlasting blessings.
The office of Moses was but typical, and he himself
needed the mediation of the Saviour whom he
foretold.

In our "One Mediator" all types end, all prophecies centre, all fulness dwells, and He is Himself
the remedy for every human woe. "One" only
Mediator—were He a less glorious being—would be
insufficient for a sin-stricken world ; but when the
"One Mediator" is the Lord of Glory, the wearied
heart may well be "abundantly satisfied."

Let us then in all times of need, when the heart is
fearful and the night seems dark ; when life per-

---

* Ps. cx. 1.　　† Isa. ix. 6.　　‡ Heb. viii. 6.

plexes or death alarms; when troubles are in the
house, or tumults in the world, come with an earnest
confiding trust to that unseen, yet near Redeemer,
who is exalted at the right hand of the Father as
our "One Mediator."

OUR PEACE.

Ephesians ii. 14.

Peace is a beautiful word, suggesting a long
succession of soothing and happy images. The
first glimpse we have of man's state is indeed one of
perfect peace within the blissful enclosure of Paradise. Soon that golden age passed away, and six
thousand years have listened to the sounds of war.
Yet, amidst the notes of strife, voices have been
heard speaking of peace regained, and man restored
to more than his original blessedness. "The Prince
of Peace"* was the expressive title given to the
future restorer of all things, eight centuries before
His appearance among men. The angels who sang
that grand hymn at the birth of the Lord, made
"peace on earth" an important part of their
triumphant praise. Among the last bequests received by the sorrowing disciples, was the rich gift
conveyed by the loving words, "Peace I leave with
you."†

* Isa. ix. 6.   † John xiv. 27.

The boon remained with them, creating in each heart a heaven, though all around was storm, and making the weakest among them a hero in the great warfare. This privilege was not restricted to the Apostles. St. Paul, speaking in the name of the whole Church, calls the Saviour "Our Peace." He reminds the Gentile converts of their former spiritual wretchedness, as "those having no hope and without God in the world," and then ascribes their recovery to Christ as the great peace maker of the soul.* This history of the regenerated Ephesians is *substantially* that of every Christian. They indeed may have worshipped the image of Diana in her magnificent temple, and we may from early years have conformed to the Christian usages established amongst us. This seems at the first glance to make a great distinction between the moral state of the Ephesians before conversion, and the condition of nominal Christians. Is not the great difference one of custom? "Without Christ" and "without God," is surely true in a very solemn sense, of all unregenerate men. What a lesson does our Great Teacher give us on this point, when He describes some who had wrought miracles in His name, and worshipped Him in words of adoration, and were rejected at last.† Those who do not judge according to appearance, will not therefore see any substantial spiritual difference between the Ephesian idolaters "without God," and the merely nominal Christian. All who have received the regenerating spirit will

* Ephes. ii. 13, 14.   † Matt. vii 22, 23.

I

acknowledge, with solemn recollections, that there was a time when all their actions were influenced by the questions, "What do I wish to do ?" or, "What do men wish me to do ?" They will admit that such an enthronement of the human will was a practical atheism of the heart, and therefore a real war against God. *Now* the question is, "Lord, what wilt Thou have me to do ?" the rebellion is over, and they are brought near their God, through the work of Him who is their " peace."

Both Jew and Gentile are to be united in one glorious Church, where there shall be no national law of multiplied ceremonies forming "a middle wall of partition." Then the sons of Abraham, no longer exulting in their exclusiveness, will rejoice, with the redeemed out of all nations, in the union of souls under Him who is " Our Peace." As St. Paul gladly renounced all his former pharisaical glorying in the ceremonial law, so will the whole body of the Jewish people yet see the typical and temporary nature of the Mosaic system, and receive Christ as the great peace maker between them and the Gentile nations.*

When this shall come to pass, that long expected era will surely draw near in which exiled peace shall return to the wearied world, and the rejoicing earth will hold her long promised jubilee under Him " Our Peace." Was it not of such a period the prophet spoke, when he described the destruction of wickedness, the termination of ignorance, the cessation of

* Rom. xi. 26.

war, and the great gathering of the nations round
"the ensign of the people"?* Then the circle of
the ages will be complete, and the peace instituted
in paradise shall be restored in the kingdom of
Christ. Towards this grand consummation multitudes are looking. Even men who have not as yet
received the spirit of the Gospel are asking for the
advent of a great Peace-giver. When the bells
ring out each old year, the voices of many are
heard from all lands, singing,—

> "Ring out, the thousand years of war;
> Ring in, the thousand years of peace."

Yes, it will surely come; the strife of souls against
their Maker will end : the contest of man with man
shall be over, effected by the mighty working of the
Lord " Our Peace."

All attempts to hush the storms of earth have
hitherto failed, because a true and lasting peace
must be fixed in the human heart before it can
visibly influence the great corporate masses called
nations. Until the Gospel has gained the predicted
victory over mankind, the great war-temple will
never be permanently closed. Jerusalem was called
the city of peace ; the name seems a mockery when
we remember the fearful struggles within and
without its walls, and its seventeen captures. In
like manner names of unity and fraternity may be
given to human institutions, but soon the evil spirit
of discord will prove the reality of its power.

* See Isaiah, chap. xi.

But there is a more special, a more personal sense in which Christ is "Our Peace." Can we not obtain, even here, a *consciousness* of forgiveness, arising from reliance on the sacrifice and mediation of our Lord? May we not also have a distinct and clear conviction of His hallowing presence and guiding hand, so that we are as sensible of our Saviour's nearness as a man can be of the companionship of his friend? From this wonderful indwelling of the Lord will spring a peace—holy, enduring, and strengthening: a peace which will draw us from the world to Him; from self to His cross; humbling us, but exalting the Saviour, and leading us daily to look unto Jesus as "Our Peace."

Titles of our Lord

AS

THE MASTER, RULER, AND KING.

THE MASTER.
THE LORD.
MY LORD AND MY GOD.
THE PRINCE OF LIFE.
THE KING OF THE JEWS.
THE KING OF KINGS.
THE LORD OF LORDS.

THE above seven most expressive names represent the Saviour as the great ruler of all things in heaven and in earth. As *The Master* we recognize in him the supreme lawgiver of the church; as *The Lord* we hear him saying, "all souls are mine"; and in the words *my Lord and my God* the holy

church throughout all the world reads in the confession of the apostle her own solemn creed.   As
The Prince of Life we behold Him ruling the whole
living universe; as *The King of the Jews* we recognize his mysterious relationship to, and special
dominion over, the house of Israel; the title *King
of Kings* shows Him as the source of all dominion;
and the name *Lord of Lords* exalts the Saviour as
the absolute owner and disposer of all things.

THE MASTER.

Matt. xix. 16; xxii. 16; xxvi. 18, 25, 49.   Mark ix. 5; x. 17.
Luke viii. 24; xii. 13.   John i. 38, &c.

This title of the Lord reminds us of the true
nature of the Christian life.   Every believer in
Jesus has, in reality, but *one* master, Christ in
heaven.   He may have many earthly superiors, but
he obeys them because such is the heavenly Master's
will.   His work may be of the meanest kind in the
eyes of men, but being appointed unto him by
Christ, he sees the great Master's name in every
duty, and this hallows all work.   What a dignity,
what a beauty this gives to a true Christian's daily
life !   Is he a ploughman ? this tilling of the soil
is the earthly work which Christ allots to him.   Is
he a mechanic ? he has ample opportunity for con-

scientious patience and skill. Does his occupation
require learning and intellectual power? these en-
dowments are not his own, nor to be used merely
for his country, or for the world, but for the honour
of the divine Master. Do we sufficiently realize
this great truth, that our life here is simply to do
the precise kind of work which the Lord sets
before us? What a simplicity this gives to life!
what a singleness of aim it produces!

We are in the habit of saying *my* work, or work
for *society*, work for *country*, work for the *church;*
how much higher do we rise when we call all this
His work, or work for the Lord Jesus. Then the
name " Master " has a meaning for our *hearts*, and
becomes a word of mighty power in our daily life.
" Excelsior " (higher) is the spirit-stirring motto
placed before his readers by a modern poet; but he
only mounts " higher " every day who works for a
Master in heaven.

This name;* as used in the New Testament, implies teaching, guardianship, and discipline. When,
therefore, His teaching becomes the guide of our
souls—when we commit ourselves entirely to His
keeping, and receive with joy of heart His hallowing
discipline—then is He really acknowledged as
Master. As disciples we profess ourselves to be
under His training, but do we not often reject His
mode of educating us for heaven, and learn other
lessons? Happy are we, indeed, when we have
learned to distinguish the Master's voice amid all

* Διδάσκαλος and Επιστάτης.

the discordant sounds of earth. But this quickness
of the spiritual ear is not easily acquired; yet if we
have it not, many a sublime lesson, many a heavenly
whisper, will have no meaning for us. There is a
possibility of sitting long in Christ's school, and yet
learning very little. Let us come nearer to the
Master, and not sit afar off. Faith, prayer, meditation, and obedience, will gradually enable us to
understand at least a little of His all-wise discipline.

Great are the varieties of the training through
which the Master leads his people. Some are tried
in spirit; doubts, perplexities, and dark sugges-
tions assail the understanding and the heart. Others
are tried in body; years of suffering make a load
of physical agony which would press the wearied
soul to the earth, were not the Master's voice heard
saying, "It is I, be not afraid." Some are tried
and taught by various losses. One looks round for
children, relatives, and friends, but sees only their
graves, and would be alone on the earth, but that
Christ is with him. Some lose houses, lands, and
goods, much wondering, and even for a time shaken
in faith by the storm. Gold, power, and fame test
others no less severely.

In all these modes the heavenly Master carries
on the work of preparing redeemed souls for the
house of "many mansions." Give all up to His
guidance. Receive with "meekness" His words of
wisdom, and compress faith, love, and obedience
into the question, "Lord, what wilt thou have me
to do?" The answer will be sure to come.

THE LORD.

Matt. viii. 2; xxii. 44. Rom. i. 3, &c.

Some names belong to the Creator alone; others
are given to the creature only; this title is applied
both to man and to the mighty God. The word,
especially in the Greek,* implies power, authority,
ownership, and dignity. These attributes belong
to the Eternal King, and being infinite in Him, we
call Him Lord in the highest possible sense. But
as men may also receive these qualities, to them the
same word is also applicable. We have therefore
two names which our divine Redeemer bore in
common with the creatures of His hand—Jesus and
Lord. One at least of the early disciples was called
Jesus,† and ancient learned Jews used the same
name. Thus, not only did the Saviour unite himself with man by taking human nature, but also by
adopting human names.

The title "Lord" implies *power;* and how exactly does it express the measureless might of
Christ! We read of the Saviour's power, we
meditate upon its manifestations, but how little
have we as yet realized its vastness and daily operation. The midnight stars in their silent beauty, the
amazing motions of the heavenly orbs, the stability
of this wondrous universe, the diversified richness

* Κύριος. † Col. iv. 11.

of the changing seasons, and even the tints of every summer flower, proclaim the "Lord" in His creative and preserving power.* Yet this mighty One, who holds the starry courses and the "water-floods" in His hand, uses this limitless power for *your* salvation, if you commit yourself to His keeping. His hand is put forth to you; do you cling firmly to it? Then His word is clear—you "shall never perish."† Sum up all the fearful evils which may confront you—an invisible host of tempting spirits; Satan in battle array; your own heart exceedingly treacherous; the very garrison of the soul not to be trusted; a vast army of temptations in the world; ignorance hiding the glories of the Lord from you; unbelief at one time leading you to trust yourself, at another to distrust your Saviour; and at the end of the road death stands. What a prospect is this for the soul! Nor is it a picture of the fancy; it is a real prospect of the land through which you must pass. What then is to be done? simply press forwards along the road, "looking unto Him,"‡ who will show His power at all the dangerous turnings of the way. Remember His two names, one "Jesus," expressing infinite love, the other "Lord," declaring infinite power. When the histories of earth are read, no one case will be found in which a Saviour's love and power have failed one trusting heart.

The "Lord" is a title of *authority;* He is a *living, present,* and *infallible* authority. Men have long sought such, and He stands close to each

* John i. 3. Col. i. 16, 17.   † John x. 28.   ‡ Heb. xii. 2.

Christian heart. He has already spoken in the Gospels clear, decisive, and comprehensive words of guidance; ponder them well, ponder them long; each is a treasury of divine thoughts.

This authority is speaking now by His spirit, by His ordinances, and in His providences. Is it "a still small voice"? that is the very mode in which the Most High often speaks.* Is the meaning of this still voice hard to be understood? not *usually* so to the prayerful, the watchful, and the obedient. The plainest intimation may prove "a hard saying" to the self-willed.†

The "Lord" is a name denoting *possession*. In one sense Christ is Lord of all—"all things that the Father hath are mine"‡—and this will make Him possessor of all, from the earth to the remotest star, which as yet no telescope has detected. But in a very peculiar sense He is the Lord of redeemed and regenerated souls. The seals of His owner-ship are four. On all the seals of creation and preservation are set. The third seal, that of re-demption, is placed on the human family. The fourth seal, that of the regenerating spirit,§ is on all true disciples of the "Lord." These, there-fore, belong to Christ in a manner peculiar to them-selves. Happy, and strong, and wise are they who can rightly hold the two grand truths—"ye are Christ's," and "all things are yours."‖

This name is expressive of the *honour* due to

---

* 1 Kings xix. 12. † John vi. 60. ‡ John xvi. 15. § Eph. i. 13.
‖ 1 Cor. iii. 22 and 23.

Christ. The Gospel narratives show how the name
"Lord" was given to Him during His sojourn
among men: in every case it was a word of honour.
But long before Jesus appeared on the earth, this
title was given by prophets to Him. David, in
spirit, "called Him Lord" ;* and Isaiah, in prophetic vision, saw the heavenly host adoring, and
heard the solemn words of their worship as the
bright seraphim cried, "Holy, holy, holy, is the
Lord of Hosts."† The hour is coming, when
either in fear or in love, the whole universe, the
sinless angels, the demons who have tried to lead
men from God, and all the generations of mankind,
shall acknowledge this title.‡

It is even now the privilege of all disciples to
commit their weak footsteps to His powerful guidance, to submit their wills to His authority, to
acknowledge their souls to be His "purchased possession," to regard every duty of life as his work,
to make every day His day, and every place His
temple. Then will He indeed be *our* "Lord," and
we shall be His "peculiar people."§

MY LORD AND MY GOD.

John xx. 28.

Many an amazing proof of the Lord's power was
given to the Apostles. They lived in the midst of

---

* Ps. cx. 1 ; and Matt. xxii. 43.   † Compare Isa. vi. 1, 3, 10, with
John xii. 39—41.   ‡ Phil. ii. 11.   § Titus ii. 14.

miracles. By the crowded porches of Bethesda's pool they beheld one marvellous work;* by a city gate a funeral procession offers to their gaze a life restored;† and in the desert wilds the five barley loaves grew mysteriously before their eyes into food for five thousand men!‡ What a singularly blessed life was enjoyed by those Apostles! To be always so near Christ—sitting with Him at table, listening to His words, and hearing His prayers. The very tones of the Redeemer's voice fell hourly upon their ears; the features of the Lord's countenance were daily before them. Sometimes we get a glimpse of the deep emotions which agitated their hearts when the glory of the Godhead flashed upon their astonished view. Many such hours there must have been, during the three years which they passed with Christ; but the veil is not very often raised, and we can but faintly imagine the mysterious blessedness of their life with Him.

One impressive incident we have now before us. On the eighth day after the resurrection of the Lord, a number of timid disciples were assembled. One week had elapsed since Jesus, by His divine power, entered in a mysterious manner into their closely-shut room, and gave to each the consecrating gift of the Holy Ghost. They had again met, probably in the same place, and now the doubting Thomas was with them. Again a miracle was wrought before their eyes—again the risen Lord stood before them. All received a loving salutation,

---

* John v. 2—9.   † Luke vii. 15.   ‡ John vi. 9—18.

but to one of that assembly there came a command
never given to any except to Thomas—"Reach
hither thy hand, and thrust it into my side." Such
was the strange, the overwhelming evidence, given
to the doubting Apostle. All his scepticism then
gave way, and he expressed the full assent of his
understanding, and the depth of his emotions, by
the emphatic words, "My Lord and My God."
The solemn title "God," which no created being
can take without blasphemy, was at once accepted
by the Lord. The Apostle had not, therefore, been
led by his excited feelings to misapply the name of
the Most High.

What a mystery is here! He who was baptized
of John, who hid Himself from the angry men of
Nazareth,* who escaped being stoned by exasperated
Jews,† was insulted by Herod's soldiers,‡ scorned
by a tumultuous mob,§ scourged as a despised slave,||
put to death with thieves,¶ and laid by a few
despised friends in a rock tomb,** He was "God"!
No man could receive such a mystery did not his
faith rest upon a mass of decisive and supernatural
evidence. As Thomas, though doubtful before, was
fully convinced when he clearly saw the Lord before
him, so will all doubt be over when the Saviour
shall show Himself in the glory of His second
coming to the assembled nations of the earth.
There will be no more scepticism after such a manifestation.

* Luke iv. 29—30. † John viii. 59. ‡ Luke xxiii. 11. § Luke xxiii. 18.
|| John xix. 1. ¶ Mark xv. 27. ** Mark xv. 46, 47.

In the meantime, let us often ponder on this great "mystery of godliness." Our Saviour is our God, then all is safe; the church is secure of victory; every soul bearing the mark of Jesus, and clinging to Him, is safe. The love which brought the Lord to the cross, is combined with the power which called up the stars from nought, and with the wisdom which has arranged all parts of this universe. Remember the marvellous words, applied to the whole body of believers by one who spoke under the guidance of the Lord—"The church of God, which He hath purchased with His own blood."* This is above all human understanding fully to grasp. The words seem almost too awful for utterance; but the Apostle uses them boldly, and we may do the same.

We shall, by meditating on the divinity of our Lord and Saviour, gain a deeper conviction of the unspeakable, the infinite value of all He did and suffered. The blood shed on the cross is called "precious,"† but who shall measure its efficacy? The Apostle, when contemplating this mysterious and perfect offering for the "sins of the whole world," asks, with all the holy confidence of faith, "Who is he that condemneth?"‡ and silences all accusation by one short but decisive answer, "It is Christ that died!" This reply is, indeed, sufficient at all times for those who give themselves up to the Saviour. There is no room for despair at the foot of the cross. If a repentant and believing sinner

* Acts xx. 28.   † 1 Peter i. 19.   ‡ Romans viii. 84.

should come there black with all the sins committed by all the fallen angels, added to every crime which earth has known, the plea, "It is Christ that died," will be a sufficient answer to the long indictment.

But this complete sufficiency of the sacrifice arises from the divine nature of the sacrificer. Let each Christian, therefore, when faith is hesitating, when love is enfeebled by remembrance of repeated sins, and hope fears to soar aloft, cast himself before the Lord with all the earnest conviction of the Apostle, flinging aside every doubt, and saying, "My Lord and My God."

THE PRINCE OF LIFE.

Acts. iii. 15.

When walking in some sequestered country church-yard at the close of a summer's day, as the setting sun sheds a subdued but golden light over the grassy mounds and moss-covered tombs, we feel the solemn, the peculiar stillness belonging to this home of many generations. All those sleeping ones were wakeful once; a busy life of many years preceded this quietude. As we gaze, the chilling shadow of a mighty destroyer seems to fall upon every grave; we feel that life is weak, and death is mighty.

But then to the ear of faith, comes a message like music from the heavens, whispering to the sorrow-

stricken heart the grand title of the " Prince of Life."
Death is therefore but a temporary conqueror ; some
victories he has gained, but the great war is not yet
over ; the hour of everlasting triumph approaches
when not one grave shall keep its tenant, for all
" the dead shall hear the voice of the Son of God."*
Christ being the " Prince of Life," has power to
stop at any moment the reign of death. We, in our
ignorance of His plan of government, may sometimes
wonder that He permits death to rule for a single
day. Be still, and wait " the salvation of the Lord."†
Earth shall yet be without a grave, and the word
" mortal," which has so fitly described every human
being, shall be no longer applicable to any of Adam's
race ; " this mortal must put on immortality."‡ To
realize this great truth, is very difficult for us who
are surrounded on every side by the signs of death.
In the crowded streets of our cities, and in the
centres of commercial life, the signs of mourning tell
of recently opened graves. How can we believe
that all this shall cease ? By looking unto Jesus as
" the Prince of Life," and receiving into an undoubt-
ing heart the grand declaration, that " death is
swallowed up in victory."§ If our faith be strong,
the very symbols of mortality will turn our gaze
towards Him, whose glorious work it will be to
liberate from their ancient prisons, the numberless
captives of " the king of terrors." How completely
had the Apostle realized the truth of this, when he

* John v. 25.   † Exodus xiv. 13.   ‡ 1 Cor. xv. 53.
§ 1 Cor. xv. 54.

K

sang that hymn of Christian triumph, "O death, where is thy sting? O grave, where is thy victory?"* Why may not we exult in like manner? He had before him the prospect of a cruel death from heathen persecutors, but his world-conquering faith made him victorious. Are we not also disciples of the same Redeemer? Then let us honour our Saviour by a like bright hope and unshaken confidence. How can He be to us "the Prince of Life," if we confess by our unbelieving fears that death is still unconquered?

How startling is the contrast between the title "Prince of Life," and the declaration that He was "killed."† This glorious One submitted to die, that He might break the bars of the grave, and so assure us of His absolute mastery over death. Others had been raised from the dead, but they came forth solely as liberated subjects of "The Prince;" He rose as the Lord who holds "the keys of hell and of death."‡

At present, and for a period fixed in the eternal counsels, "the Prince of Life" refrains from fully exercising His dominion over the grave. A few more ages may pass before the progress of death shall be stayed, but every day brings nearer the bright hour when the divine injunction will proclaim "there shall be no more death."§ Then the triumphant church, gathered out of every land, shall witness the completion of the Lord's great and enduring victory. In that crisis of human history,

* 1 Cor. xv. 55. † Acts iii. 15. ‡ Rev. i. 18. § Rev. xxi. 4.

men shall comprehend the deep and emphatic meaning contained in the expressive title, "the Prince of Life."

In the meantime, the Saviour is keeping in a blessed and holy security those who sleep in Him. Above their quiet graves the storms of time may rage, but no murmur of the tempest disturbs their calm and hallowed rest.

How quietly are their perfect spirits awaiting the unfolding of their loving Lord's purposes. Their bodies may be entirely dissolved, every atom separated from its kindred atom, but in joyful confidence they look for the hour when the ruined temple shall be rebuilt; while Satan, rebellious human spirits, the redeemed multitudes, and the glorious ranks of the unfallen angels, shall witness the amazing restoration.

To what an event are we gradually approaching? The wheels of time may stop to-morrow, or they may roll onwards for many ages; but let each Christian with faith, hope, and love, all in holy watchful action, be looking out for the day when the groans of creation* shall cease at the coming of "the Prince of Life."

* Rom. viii 22.

THE KING OF THE JEWS.

Matt. ii. 2; xxvii. 37.   Mark xv. 12, 18   Luke xxiii. 3, 38.
John xviii. 33; xix. 19.

The sceptre had departed from Judah, the glory
of the royal line of the Maccabees was extinguished,
its last Princess, Mariamne, had been married to the
cruel Idumæan Herod, and executed by his orders.
The heathen Roman appointed and deposed the high
priests of Judah at his pleasure.*   The walls of the
holy city had been broken by the battering rams of
Pompey, and the Holy of holies itself had been
entered by the Roman general.   But amidst this
national humiliation an inquiry is heard even from
the East, "Where is He that is born King of the
Jews?"   The early representatives of the Gentile
world are seeking the new-born King.

Though "laid in a manger," the "King of the
Jews" was not without honour.   The representatives
of the whole earth came to that manger; the shepherds of Bethlehem did homage for the Jews, the
"wise men" worshipped for the Gentiles.†   This

* Between the return from Babylon and the destruction of Jerusalem
by the Romans, four dynasties ruled over the Jews. The Persians, the
Greek kings of Syria, the Maccabees, and the line of Herod.

† Gold and spices were the customary offerings to Eastern kings.
St. Matthew, with evangelic brevity, simply calls them "wise men."
Tradition became daring, not only giving the number three, but even
the names, Gaspar, Melchior and Balthazar, and making Cologne their
burial place.

was an early foreshadowing of the honour which the "King of the Jews" shall, at the appointed time, receive from all people. The angels sang "glory in the highest," the shepherds spread the wonderful news over their hills and vales, the men of the East poured out their treasures; and what of the Jewish nation? The rumour that the "King" had come, "troubled" all Jerusalem; but it was the trouble of infidel rulers and a heartless people. Their learned doctors could direct the wise men to the royal presence chamber; it would have seemed natural had every priest, scribe, and Levite then in Jerusalem followed with eager haste to Bethlehem. There is no evidence that even one went to see whether "the King of the Jews" had come.

This was a new kind of kingship. The glory was so strangely hidden; veiled by so many coverings from the gaze of men. The birth in the manger, the lowly social position of Joseph, the mechanical occupation, the absence of school learning,* the seclusion of Nazareth, the poverty of His mature life,† the low rank of His immediate associates, the hatred of the powerful, and the awful ignominy of the crucifixion. Who, unless by a Divine illumination, could see "the King" through all these coverings of humiliation? Poor human judgment decides according to appearances, and terrible are its mistakes. "The King of the Jews" was unknown to the narrow-minded Jew, the subtle Greek, or the power loving Roman.

* John vii. 15. † Matt viii. 20; xvii. 27.

What happened in the days of His earthly sojourn
to "the King" Himself, may befal His followers
now. They, too, are "kings,"* but their kingly
rank is hidden. Men may pass one of these in the
crowded streets; he may be poor, a mechanic, an
unlearned, and they know him not.

But the glory of "the King" was not always
hidden. The power and majesty often shone through
the veils. The souls and bodies of men; the animal
and vegetable kingdoms; the winds and the waters;
the rage of demons and the secret thoughts of
enemies, acknowledged His sway. Impressed by
these manifestations of glory, the fickle multitude
did, for a few hours, hail Him as their King, when
the shout of "Hosanna"† rose over the towers of
Jerusalem. Even the children took up the popular
cry,‡ and it seemed as if the Jews were about to
acknowledge the "King." But even then the Lord
saw the infuriate crowd which would soon cry,
"Crucify Him," and wept over the coming doom of
the populous city. "The King of the Jews" was
acknowledged by the Saviour as His special title
when questioned by the sceptical Pilate;|| and this
admission drew forth the mockery of the licentious
Herod, the insult of the "gorgeous" robe, and the
dreadful irony of the thorny crown. Each one of
these scorners will, at a future day, bow down before

---

* Rev. i. 6.

† This word means "Save, we pray," and was taken from Psalm
cxviii. 25.

‡ Matt. xxi. 15. || Luke xxiii. 3.

that despised title. The very men who platted the
thorns, those who forced the crown of pain upon
that sacred head, they who brought forth the robe
of mockery, will see the King in His glory.

"King of the Jews" was the title affixed to the
cross. In Hebrew the Jew read it, in Latin the
Roman remembered it, and in Greek the words were
carried into many a distant land. This name of our
Lord is, therefore, peculiarly distinguished. It was
given at His birth, used at His crucifixion, uttered
by disciples, adopted by enemies, and acknowledged
by the Redeemer Himself.

THE KING OF KINGS.

Rev. xix. 16.

High and mighty names are given by men to the
conquerors or rulers of nations. Even death does
not hush the loud sounding epithets; the tombs bear
the inscriptions, and history hands down to distant
ages the lofty titles of buried potentates. No wonder
that the men of earth should, sometimes, have regarded the possessors of so much visible magnificence
as beings of a race superior to mortals, and should
have raised altars and temples to their honour. Yet
these mighty ones were only *depositaries* of power,
not its fountain head; mere trustees of a higher
Ruler; permitted deputies of a supreme invisible
Power. Such is man's tendency to worship the

creature, and neglect the Creator, that a Nero, a Caligula, or a Domitian was feared, while "the King of kings" was forgotten. How strange that a being so mighty should permit Himself to be hidden by His own feeble creatures.

This magnificent title, "King of kings," presents to our minds another of those amazing contrasts in which the history of man's redemption abounds. To the infant of Bethlehem, to the child of twelve years conversing with the doctors in the temple, and to the crucified of Calvary, this name of supreme authority belongs. The contrast between the manger at Bethlehem, and the grandeur described in the 19th chapter of Revelation, is so wonderful, that nothing but the express speaking of the Holy Spirit could make our faith in such a mystery seem reasonable.

This title directs our contemplation to the *supreme authority* over all men and all worlds which has been committed to the eternal Son. His own parting words to His worshipping disciples, "All power is given unto Me in heaven and in earth,"* contain a similar idea. We are therefore justified in holding that our Redeemer is the true and supreme, though for the present invisible, King of this world. All powers, whatsoever be their pretensions, exist either by His appointment or permission. When we hail our Lord as "King of kings," we are not using mere oriental imagery, or bold figures of speech, but employing the simplest language possible to express

* Matt. xxviii. 18.

a grand fact. Many evil powers may be permitted, for awhile, to domineer over the earth, and Satan is called " the Prince of the power of the air,"* but these usurpations are but temporary. The time is approaching when " the kingdoms of this world " shall yield themselves to the only true King. Even now the Lord is King; restraining or turning to His own ends the counsels of princes, senates, and statesmen. They may be ignorant of His secret, ever-working influence; they may even deride the idea of such a controling power; but the Lord's anointed is seated on the " holy hill," and whether " the people imagine a vain thing," or " the rulers take counsel together," the eternal purposes shall be accomplished. Let us not be led by high-sounding phrases about " laws of nature," of which we know so little, to forget the doctrine of a Divine oversight of all things, which the Great Teacher suggested, when He reminded His disciples that even a sparrow did not die without the cognizance of the Creator.†

" The Lord is King," then let our hearts be tranquil, our trust steady, our hopes bright, and our labour stedfast. We are doing the Great King's work, on the King's own ground, and according to His directions. We cannot see into the future; surely that need not perplex us; it all lies mapped out before Him. We cannot ensure results; the King does not expect that from any of His people; obedience is ours, the issues are with Him.

But this supreme authority of " the King of

* Eph. ii. 2.   † Matt. x. 29.

kings " extends beyond earth ; the " all power " is
exercised in heaven, where the Saviour rules over
the hosts of the saved, and over the celestial principalities and dominions.* If we sometimes think the
Lord's kingdom on the earth is but small, let us not
forget that countless multitude of invisible spirits,
both human and angelic, over which He reigns.
The services they render are unknown to us, but
they probably as far transcend ours, as the work of
the greatest philosopher excels the reasoning of a
child.

Imagination cannot grasp the grandeur of our
Lord's kingship ; the few intimations lead us to
adore, but forbid us to speculate. Surely a Christian ·
must exult in the thought that the Holy One, who
submitted to the tortures of the Cross for our redemption, is even now so gloriously exalted. We
have committed the keeping of our souls not only to
the loving, sympathising Son of Man, but to the
mighty " King of kings."

But we must not forget that this authority of
Christ extends even to the fallen angels. When on
earth He checked their power by many a miracle of
love to men, and He now holds " the keys of hell."†
For a time these malicious spirits are allowed some
liberty ; the reason for this we know not yet ; but
we are assured that all their counsels shall not prevail against the redeemed of the Lord.‡ Let each
believer, who is trusting in and obeying Jesus,
rejoice that all the subtlety, malice, and power of

* Eph. i. 21.; Heb. i. 6.   † Rev. i. 18.   ‡ Matt. xvi. 18.

the whole satanic host will be unable to destroy those whom the "King of kings" shelters.

Thus over the three worlds of men, angels, and demons, the Saviour has "all power." The full majesty of His kingly glory is not yet revealed to us; at the appointed time the King will come, the day of His recognition by the whole Creation is ap-approaching, when the "many crowns"* shall symbolize the adoration given by all orders of intelligent beings. This day of the Saviour's coronation every eye shall witness; how unutterable will be the emotions of that mighty host; how tremendous the results to some, how transcendently glorious to many. Such a day will be a fit climax to the wonderful history of this world, when all miracles, all prophecies, all revelation, all history, shall be concentrated in one grand closing event, the manifestation, in glory, of the "King of kings."

THE LORD OF LORDS.

Rev. xix. 16.

As the title "King of kings," declares the supreme *authority* possessed by the Son, so the designation "Lord of lords," proclaims Him the appointed *possessor* of a far-extended domain. The words of Jesus to His disciples, "all things that the Father hath are mine,"† direct us to the same truth; and

* Rev. xix. 12.   † John xvi. 15.

the Apostle calls on all believers to contemplate the
Saviour as the " appointed heir of all things."*

Let none therefore fear, lest in thus exalting the
Son they are offending against the glory of the
Father. We are but obeying our heavenly Teacher,
who has so clearly declared that " all men should
honour the Son, even as they honour the Father."†
Reason might infer that He by whom " all things
were made,"‡ for whom " all things were created,"
and by whom " all things consist,"§ must be the
supreme possessor of all worlds. Under Him therefore, and from Him at His pleasure, all beings,
authorities, and dominions, hold as tenants. Nations,
princes, kings, and emperors, may call large portions
of the earth their own, and in practice exclaim,
" who is Lord over us "?‖ An answer is often given
to this presumptuous boast, when the "Lord of
lords " puts down the mighty from their seats,"¶ and
ejects the proudest holders from their temporary
possessions.

The Christian who fully comprehends the exaltation of his Saviour, will look upon all things as the
inheritance of Christ. The distant stars, the light
from which takes centuries to reach the earth, are
within the limits of the Redeemer's dominion. They
are included in the "all things," which " consist,"
or " hold together,"** under His controling power.
Thus the discoveries of the astronomer may aid the
believer in his attempts to. realize the " glory "

* Heb. i. 2.   † John v. 23.   ‡ John i. 3.   § Col. i. 16, 17.
‖ Ps. xii. 4.   ¶ Luke i. 52.   ** Col. i. 17.

which belongs to the Son. All terrestrial scenes, all celestial phenomena, are associated with the name of Jesus, to whom, as "Lord of Lords," the worlds belong. Wherever our home may be, we can always feel that we are on the Lord's domain ; the splendour and the pomp of time are His to allot to whomsoever He may please. Perhaps, Christian, you are some-times amazed that the great proprietor gives so many a glittering treasure to those who reject Him, rather than to those who love Him. You see not the hidden balances of eternity in which the Lord weighs these earthly things. The value He sets on them may be partly learned from His life, when dwelling with men. The silver and the gold were His, yet He left them to such as Herod and Pilate, while He had not money sufficient to pay a small Jewish tax. A miracle was wrought, and the money thus procured amounted to about three shillings only.* The power which so obtained that coin,† could in a moment have accumulated riches beyond all precedent. If the Lord chose poverty for Himself when on earth, is it a marvel that He sometimes allots it to His disciples now. Let us wait His time without a murmuring thought. The "Lord of lords" has all things at His disposal ; if He withhold any, shall we in our ignorance deem Him unwise or unkind ? His treasure houses will be opened in due time for all His faithful people, but "patient waiting"‡ must be their motto.

As "Lord of lords," Christ is the supreme

* Matt. xvii. 24, 27. † A Stater. ‡ 2 Thess. iii. 5.

depository of all spiritual blessings, in whom " all fulness "* dwells, and to whom therefore every renewed heart turns for necessary supplies of grace.

All other fountains are filled from Him, and would soon become exhausted, but " of His fulness," the souls of holy men in all ages have received, and ever shall receive, the true unction of the heart. To enumerate these heavenly treasures which the " Lord of lords " holds by right at His disposal, is impossible ; a life of faith on the Son of God will best make them known, and enable the enriched heart to appreciate in some degree, the abounding grace stored up in the " fulness of the Godhead."† If His dominion as " Lord of lords " over the universe baffles all our attempts to comprehend its extent, let us be assured the gifts of grace are without limit. His creative and preserving power obtained the former ; His redeeming love, incomprehensible sufferings, and wonderful death, purchased the latter. He has received " gifts for men,"‡ which for value, variety, suitability, fulness, and duration, must far transcend the utmost reach of our imagination. One standard by which we measure them we do indeed see, the price paid for them. But who shall state the value of that price ? The Apostle calls it " precious,"§ but makes no further attempt to measure the immeasurable.

We look for great things hereafter, may we not expect great blessings now ? " Come unto Me,"

* Col. i. 19.   † Col· ii. 9.   ‡ Ps. lxviii. 18.   § 1 Peter i. 19.

are the words of Him, whose possessions are infinite.
Let us then draw near, since He bids us; let us ask
great things for our own souls, great things for the
world, glorious things for the Church; for is not He
to whom we pray, limitless in power as in love?
Surely faith may satisfy her most ardent expectations,
when she petitions the " Lord of lords."

---◆---

𝔗itles of our 𝔏ord

AS

THE DAILY BREAD OF THE SOUL,

AND

THE FOUNTAIN OF LIVING WATER.

---◆---

THE BREAD OF LIFE.
THE SPIRITUAL ROCK.

THESE two titles lead us to look to the Saviour as the origin of all that sustains and refreshes the soul. We see in *The Bread of Life* the Divine energy which quickens day by day the wearied spirit of man ; and from *The Spiritual Rock* is ever flowing those waters which make " glad the city of God."

THE BREAD OF LIFE.

John vi. 35—48.

A great struggle is going on every day in all parts of the earth, and has been continued through all ages. What is its object? Not riches; for the great mass of mankind never expect them. Not fame, for which the toiling millions do not strive; not scientific knowledge, whose beauties and difficulties are unknown to the multitude. The object is "Bread." To obtain food for the body is the motive which moves nearly all human labour. That is the work to which each rising sun calls every land. Let the food of a people fail, and the whole system of the national life is paralyzed. The wisdom of laws, the sagacity of statesmen, and the fascinating richness of art and genius are of no avail. A loaf is worth them all. This absorbing struggle is to preserve the life of the body for a few years.

Does man's soul require bread? In other words, is something needed to keep it from decline and from death? What food is to the body, truth, right motives, a knowledge of itself and of its God, is to the soul. Without food the body dies; that is, it and the soul are separated; without heavenly truth the soul dies, or, is separated from God, which is spiritual death. But where can the soul get bread? "I am the Bread of Life" is the answer from the great Lord of Life.

When the Lord proclaimed Himself by this expressive title, He contrasted the "bread from heaven" with the manna.* The men who had eaten that, so many ages before, were dead; but there is a bread which a man may eat "and not die." This is undoubtedly the "bread of life," and the startled Jews might justly pray, "Lord, evermore give us this bread."† "The staff of life" is a common expression for our bodily food, but the staff falls from each dying hand after a few years, proving how little truth is in the description. The soul that receives Christ, His truth, His influences, and His complete Gospel, "shall never see death."‡ Such words have a deep reality of meaning in them. Some minds, from often hearing such sentences, come to regard them as poetic or highly wrought descriptions of the Gospel blessings. But the Great Teacher dealt in no sentimentalities; the mysteries of the future world were open to His view, and every word He uttered contains truth most momentous for us, though in some respects far beyond our grasp. The soul may *die* without being annihilated, and to prevent this the "bread of life" is offered.

As the manna came from above, being in no way dependent on Jewish labour or skill, so does "the bread of God."§ The holy truths by which Christ gives life to the soul, are as utterly unconnected with any system of man's devising, as the manna was independent of ploughman or sower. Strange

* John vi. 32.   † John vi. 34.   ‡ John viii. 51.
§ John vi. 33.

indeed would it have been if "the bread of life" had come from a world of death. They who eat of this bread partake therefore of heavenly, even of a divine food, and are fitted for a high and glorious life.*

We pray for "daily" food, because we need such, and this "bread of life" must also be continually received. The soul requires its daily supplies, and without them will be unfitted for the incessant battle or the continued race. While life is working bread is wanted.†

Strength is a mystery, but the most ignorant admit its connection with our food; and the "bread of life" must impart a superhuman power. The world sings loud praises in honour of its strong children, the men of renown, and the mighty ones of time. Great is the mistake often made in such judgments. These great ones are often weak ones. The lord of millions may be the slave of wickedness; the conqueror of nations may be the subdued of Satan. Some may indeed have been giants, but a small foe often overthrew them. The bread of earth imparts the strength of earth; but, to be strong against the ruler of the darkness of this world, we must eat "the bread of life."

A sufficiency of this heavenly food can always be obtained. Enough is offered, but what if only a

---

* The shewbread was called "Bread of the Presence," or, as in our version, "Before the Lord," (1 Sam. xxi. 6) reminding us that all divine food prepares the soul for the divine presence.

† The twelve loaves of the shewbread, being renewed every Sabbath, was called the "continual bread." Numb. iv. 7.

slight repast be taken ?   Then will follow decline in
spiritual energy, a torpor of the heart, and the
symptoms of a feverish and irregular life.   In such
a condition the mind seeks for false stimulants, runs
after sensations, and turns from " the bread of
life " to the gilded and sweetened poisons which
form the feasts of earth.

" The bread of life," like the manna, is a mystery.
The Israelites knew not the nature of the food which
fell around their tents.   " What is it ?" was their
question of surprise.   And who understands how
believers are made one with Christ, or the mode in
which the Gospel truths operate when changing
sinful men into " saints in light ?"

But " the bread of life " can be received without
comprehending the mystery of its working.   Let us
be sure that we are daily partaking of the holy food
by faith ; let us not be so deluded as to substitute
husks for bread, or man's food for Christ's feast.

" The bread of life " will be everlastingly needed.
Never will the period come when the redeemed will
be able to live without the presence of their Lord ;
for ever He will be not only the source of joy, but
the stay of life.   The Jewish shewbread was renewed
weekly ; being of the earth it decayed, though resting on the golden table, but the eternal bread abides
for ever, an infinite supply in the Paradise of God.

THE SPIRITUAL ROCK.

1 Cor. x. 4.

The Holy Spirit revealed the glories of the Messiah to the ancient Israelites by three modes of teaching—prophecy, types, and history. Thus by words, signs, and events, was Christ preached to the Jews of old. For us also who have a brighter light there lies many a deep, many a heavenly lesson in the historical parts of the Old Testament. To some these narratives may tell little, except of struggles amid the hills of Palestine, or the sands and rocks of the desert, which can have little interest for Christians in the nineteenth century. Not so, however, did St. Paul read the solemn story of ancient Israel's life. He saw in these histories, " admonitions " and " examples "* for the believers of his own day; and what these facts were to the Christians of the first century, they are to us. The Apostle beheld in the rock which poured forth cooling streams in the burning desert, a representation of our Lord, and calls it a symbolical or " spiritual rock."

When the hosts of Israel came to Rephidim,† a great want was felt—" there was no water." From the vast multitude one eager cry arose— " Give us water, that we may drink." The need was real; the cry was earnest. How exactly did

* 1 Cor. x. 6, 11.   † Exod. xvii. 1.

the state of the Jewish host represent the natural
condition of mankind! The world has, from the
beginning, felt a great want; every false religion is
but an attempt of the erring heart to satisfy its
craving. Men may wonder that the pagan should
worship a stone: it would be a greater wonder
were he content without any worship at all. The
world had wandered far from " the fountain of
living waters," but sin could not extinguish the
craving for something instead. Nor is this the state
of heathens only. Look at the educated, intellectual, but unchristian minds of the present age.
How intense is the desire for a something—a speculation, a system, or a philosophy that shall fill the
spiritual void. But " there is no water."

" Rephidim " is thought by many to have been a
place where water was usually found: there was
therefore a grievous disappointment added to a
severe want. Here again we see an apt emblem of
man and his hopes, when these are fixed upon
merely earthly sources of good. How often has
humanity been disappointed in its expectations of
help from some great one! Let any thoughtful
man glance at the imposing schemes propounded
during the last hundred years; some professing to
supersede the Gospel, others ignoring all divine aid.
Much was expected, but what has been the result?
May not many a vexed unbeliever cry out with in-
dignation, " There was no water " ?

Israel obtained their desire, but the stream flowed
from a most unusual source. The spring was not

found in some fertile oasis—some vale rich with verdure—but in a sunburnt rock in Horeb.* Is not this descriptive of Him from whom men expected nothing great—who was regarded as "a root out of dry ground,"† despised and rejected by His own people, but who was the fountain of "everlasting life." ‡ When the Lord walked upon the earth there were many sects professing to guide men to living waters; but few of these proud inquirers came to Jesus. One turned to Plato, another to Aristotle, and the Pharisees to doctors of "old time;" but to all the Lord from heaven seemed like the dry rock.

When the thirsting people came to Rephidim, they had already journeyed through a desert, and longed for rest; but the want of water compelled all to toil onwards. What a long and wearisome march has the world already made! In six thousand years rest has not been found, nor shall it be gained until the nations sit down by the side of the living waters. The fountain has long been opened; the "spiritual rock" was stricken in times long past; the river of the city of God has been flowing ever since. Kingdoms have drank of the waters, and multitudes are now living in the green pastures near the stream. Many a road is now being opened by which the wearied tribes of earth shall approach the life-giving river.

Many there are, even in Christian lands, who are fretted into misanthropy, and even led into "the seat

* Exod. xvii. 6.   † Isaiah liii. 2.   ‡ John iv. 14.

of the scornful," by dissatisfaction with surrounding religious systems. Will such men thoughtfully, and with honesty of purpose, listen to the Gospel message, which summons the fevered heart "to the waters"?* The language is figurative, suited to man's understanding, but the blessing is real and lasting, adapted to man's wants.

Israel had already received the manna in the wilderness of Sin; this should have led them to trust their God in every difficulty; yet when they feel the want of water, the old murmuring spirit returns.† May not Christians see in this an instance of that power of unbelief which forgets past providences, and past spiritual aid, in the present trial? Many can remember stages in life's journey where they felt a solemn assurance—a conviction higher than logical proof—that a divine power was with them. Yet the next trial, it may be, shakes their confidence in the merciful guidance of the Saviour.

The flowing of the water from the rock in Horeb was accompanied by a significant and divinely-appointed action. Moses was commanded "to smite the rock" with his rod. Does not this remind us of the wonderful method by which health and life were secured for men when the Lord of Glory was "smitten of God," stricken by the soldiers, and smitten by the Roman spear? That water should not flow until the rock was smitten might have seemed strange to some of the elders of Israel : and many amongst us may marvel much

* Isaiah lv. 1 ; John vii. 37.   † Exod. xvii. 3.

that our salvation must be procured by the agony
and death of the Son of God. But as the thirsty
Israelite did not allow his wonder to prevent him
from drinking the water, so the mystery which
baffles our understanding must not keep us from
the fountain opened for sin.

The blessings which came from the rock "followed" the Israelites ; and the Redeemer keeps near
to His people. Mercies are found at every step,
like flowers of paradise upon a human path, but the
Lord scatters them on our road ; the river of life
silently flows at our side, but He directs its course ;
as we cross the desert the stream fails not, because
He is the fountain ; even into "the valley of the
shadow of death" the still waters of an endless
mercy flow, for their source is in the "spiritual
rock," and that rock is Christ.

Section VIII.

Titles of our Lord

AS

THE GUIDE AND INTERCESSOR.

THE SHEPHERD.
THE BISHOP OF SOULS.
THE CAPTAIN OF SALVATION.
THE ADVOCATE.
THE FAITHFUL WITNESS.

THE above titles are ever reminding us of the Lord's care over His people. As a *Shepherd*, we see Him guiding and guarding the purchased flock; as a *Bishop*, ever watching over His far-spreading church; as a *Captain*, leading the hosts of the redeemed to victory; as an *Advocate*, defending all confiding disciples against their Satanic accuser; and as *The Faithful Witness*, giving testimony to the work of His grace in every land.

THE SHEPHERD.

John x. 11.   Hebrews xiii. 20.   1 Peter ii. 25.   1 Peter v. 4.

The sheepfold in a wild region is ever in peril. The herds of cattle on the plains of Bashan can defend themselves; and even the hill-side goats repel all ordinary foes. But the solitary wolf prowls boldly near the sheepfold, fearing nothing from the sheep, and dreading only the shepherd. How completely does all this represent the condition of the church on earth !

The weak people of God are in a world where multitudes of wicked and powerful spirits are for awhile allowed to dwell. As these evil angels have probably been on the earth for about six thousand years, they must have gained a knowledge of human nature in all its vulnerable points. Had a man of common understanding lived upon the earth since the days of Adam, watching the lives of mankind, and noting all their weaknesses, his long and strange experience must have made him a master in the art of ruling men. Such knowledge, added to a singular malice and subtle intellect, is possessed by the fallen angels. The terms wolf and lion well represent the fierce nature of these spirits, while the word sheep as clearly intimates the weak-

ness of even the holiest men in the presence of
such foes. This being the state of Christ's followers, and such the permitted might of Satan, the
question arises, How can the church escape destruction ? The wolves must conquer in a war with the
sheep. To this conclusion some men seem very
gladly to have come, declaring that Christianity
must pass away, and give place to some other
system. How do we know they are wrong ? Because Christ, the mighty Lord, who has described
His church under the similitude of sheep, has proclaimed Himself as "The Shepherd." The sheepfold is not defenceless, and with such a keeper must
be safe.

There are two classes of shepherds, those who
watch for hire, and those who keep their own
flocks. Our Lord is the owner of the flock He
protects; having bought them with a price, which
shepherd never paid before—His own blood !

The sheep may feed in lands where the mighty of
the earth rule, but these are not the lords of the
sheepfold. There may be many under-shepherds
superintending the flocks, but these are not its
owners. Times have indeed been when certain
under-shepherds took upon themselves to put their
own names on the sheep, but the Great Shepherd
came and restored His own mark.

The Lord is "the Good Shepherd," and one of
the qualities of such must be *gentleness*. Most
beautifully was this characteristic of the Saviour
described by the prophet more than seven hun-

dred years before the Holy One appeared on the earth.*

The full depth of the Redeemer's tenderness has never been apprehended by us. He who formed the innumerable starry hosts, who directs the amazing motions of planets and comets in their far-projected orbits, and who will judge all mankind, is surrounded with such a sublimity of glory, that we at first stand afar off in fear and wonder. But when we see Him in human form, walking amid the homes of the lowly, restoring health to fever-stricken patients, speaking words of pity to wounded spirits, and gladdening the hearts of even little children, then we begin to understand a little of the gentleness of infinite love — then we see how appropriate is the title " Good Shepherd."

This tenderness is often shown in a way which seems stern to the flock. The sheep become restive ; some daring one tries to break out of the fold, all follow, and when the Shepherd drives the silly wanderers back, they think Him severe. How often has the history of Christ's people exhibited such interpositions ! The church, in whole or in part, has become corrupted—is breaking bounds : the Shepherd from His high post marks the peril, and sends forward, as a warning or a check, some sharp visitation. Not His want of gentleness, but the flock's tendency to wander, brought the infliction.

A good shepherd is as *watchful* as gentle. But he who watches the fold must not be far off. The

* Isaiah xl. 11.

nearness of Christ to the church is one of those
fundamental facts which the world ignores, and
Christians often forget. "I am with you alway"*
is a truth to be most assuredly realized by all
faithful churches, and by every true Christian.
Sometimes a whole flock of sheep will break from
the fold in the middle of a dark night, and dart off
in different directions. Shall the headstrong flock
be left to die in the mountain wastes? We hear
the Shepherd saying, His sheep "shall never
perish,"† and all are brought back again. The
Christian can mark many an eventful chapter in
the history of the church where such spiritual resto-
rations of whole communities are recorded. In
our land, in Germany, France, and Switzerland,
those who have eyes to see may note such instances.

But some may ask, "If the Shepherd be thus
watchful and ever present, how can damage ever
happen to any part of the fold? How has it come
to pass that some folds have been destroyed?" Let
us not mistake the Shepherd's work. He may
remove a fold from a region which has become unfit
for it, but this is not destruction. The folds of the
Lord are not necessarily fixed, but resemble those
in Eastern countries, where flocks are removed from
one district to another, and where some pastures are
wholly abandoned. Such flocks are not destroyed;
such shepherds are not unwatchful. A stranger
passing through the deserted plains might suppose
the sheep had perished, when they have only been
removed.

* Matt. xxviii. 20.   † John x. 28.

There are lands where Christian churches once
flourished, and in which now the Gospel is almost
unknown. North Africa is one such region. These
cases are but removals, and not destructions of the
flock. The reasons for the breaking up of a fold
may be hidden in the mind of a shepherd; but
let us not imagine that any of His sheep have
perished.

Many Christians must be certain from their
own experience that a special care—an *individual*
guidance—is vouchsafed by the heavenly Shepherd
to every one of His flock. Do all such not see
along the road of life the holy memorial stones
which mark the places where the Shepherd has met
them in His love ?

One part of a shepherd's work is to *feed* his
flock, and his skill is seen in the selection of the
best districts where his charge may " find pasture "
in all seasons. The church of Christ has lived
through many ages, and found a temporary home
in various lands. At one time persecuted by impe-
rial Rome; at another worried by petty tyrants
fiercer than Alpine wolves ;* now living amid the
snares of a voluptuous, artistic, and intellectual
age ; then placed as a lonely colony in a barbarous
and unlettered time. But amidst all these diver-
sities the necessary pastures have always been found
by the Shepherd. This has been the unfailing law for
Christ's people, whether as churches or individuals.
How clearly did the great Hebrew poet declare his

* See Histories of the Vaudois.

experience of this truth nearly three thousand years ago, in that beautiful word picture, in which "the green pastures" lie before us, and the "still waters" harmonize with the quiet landscape.* But his Shepherd is also ours, and what he enjoyed we may possess. The poorest Christian peasant on English soil, in the nineteenth century, may rest in the same spiritual pastures, and walk by the same living waters which gladdened the heart of the prophet king.

The shepherd may give food *direct* to the flock from his own hands, or he may see fit to employ various agencies. Often, without the aid of any outward means, the soul receives from her invisible, though present Lord, a solemn, hallowing influence: public worship, the faithful use of sacraments, scripture reading, works of faith, labours of love, prosperous events, or deep trials, are at other times the means by which the grace of the Saviour reaches the heart.

In all these divine dealings we see another of the Great Shepherd's modes of discipline. "He leadeth" and "goeth before" the sheep.† The manner of this guidance varies with times, countries, and circumstances, but it is a *reality*, and is every day shaping our spiritual life. Men without religion, or who hold certain notions of a providence working afar off by general laws only, may regard the doctrine of a divine, personal, and special guiding of the soul, as mere sentiment or

* Psalm xxiii. 1, 2.   † John x. 3, 4.

enthusiasm. All such should ask how the infallible teaching of our Lord can be reconciled with the denial of such influence.*

We must bear in mind that "The Shepherd" has a perfect knowledge of His sheep.† To the stranger, each one of a flock may seem like the rest, but He who is with them notes the peculiarities of each. Deep and mysterious struggles may be going on utterly unknown to us in the soul of a man with whom we constantly associate; but all the deeps of the heart's life are open to the heart's great Teacher.

But must not the Shepherd be also *known to the sheep?* This is one of the marks distinguishing the flock of Christ.‡ He is invisible, and yet He is known, because the thoughtful, prayerful, and regenerate soul is endowed with the faculty of distinguishing the presence of her Lord. The mind has an eye and an ear which may be trained to high excellence in art and science. And is there not a spiritual training by which the voice of the Divine Shepherd is recognized, and His guiding hand seen? Thus the Christian may say to the world—

> "I hear a voice you cannot hear;
> I see a hand you cannot see."

Let us not forget the final result of the great Shepherd's work—to bring all the scattered and purchased sheep from their different folds, so that there may

---

* See especially John x. 1—16; xiv. 6—23; xviii. 21—23.
† John x. 14.   ‡ John x. 4.

M

be "one fold and one shepherd."*   Then the marvellous history of time will be closed, and the whole redeemed family of God be united in that perfect harmony for which the whole creation is now looking with an intense longing.

THE BISHOP OF SOULS.

1 Peter ii. 25.

To watch over and to guide aright one human soul, is often found to be a work above the powers of a good and a wise man. After years of oversight, and a long course of patient training, one hour of rebellion frustrates the plans of a life. Who then shall guide all souls ? Many a scheme has been framed, in the hope of finding a power to control and direct the energies of millions of self-seeking, obstinate wills. Legislators, poets, priests, philanthropists, and philosophers, all promise help. Some good is thus done ; manners are perhaps refined ; higher sentiments are infused ; some loftier aims suggested, and a few noble deeds reward the efforts of so many workers. But the "souls" of men are not rescued from the paths of death. They are, indeed, following various guides, for the heart fears to go alone on a desolate road, but the leaders are themselves often lost on the dark mountains. Amidst the almost universal scattering, we do indeed see one

* John x. 16.

company toiling steadily up a narrow way, making a slow but evident progress. At their head is the banner of the Cross, and they are all looking, though with varying intentness, to One who, from the distant heights, is beckoning them onwards. Thus the Church advances, for "the Bishop of Souls" is guiding. That company alone, of all mankind, has found One to watch over them, and to watch for them.

The Apostle connects this title, "Bishop," with that of "Shepherd," and each suggests, though in different forms, the same great and comforting truth. If Christians be regarded as sheep, then their Lord is represented as a Shepherd; if they be viewed as a church, as regenerate and sanctified, needing the constant teaching of their heavenly Master, He is fitly set before them as the Overseer* or "Bishop" of souls.

A true Christian will feel how exactly such a word expresses the ceaseless watchfulness of our heavenly Lord. He alone sees the hosts of evil spirits keeping their incessant watch around the beleagured city of God ; He marks the "fiery darts" flung by satanic malice, and notes the plots of the "gates of hell."

None therefore but Himself can take the oversight of His menaced family. None can act as Christ's perfect deputy in thus watching the powers of darkness. The ordinary bishops, or overseers of the Church, are themselves subject to the "wiles" of

---

* The writer may remind some of his readers that 'Επισκοπος, whence the word bishop is derived, denotes strictly an *over-looker* or *over-seer*.

Satan, in common with others, and therefore require
for their own safety the superintending and loving
care of "the Bishop of Souls." We have here
another instance of that pre-eminence " in all
things,"* which it is the Father's purpose the
beloved Son should have. The comprehensive and
exalting title, "Bishop of Souls," belongs in its
highest sense, to the Lord alone. To Him only all
regenerate souls look for guidance, from Him alone
all receive directions. He who knows the secrets,
the weaknesses, the wants, and the dangers of all
hearts, is alone fitted to be universal Bishop. Here
is another illustration of the true unity of Christ's
Church, all branches of which are gathered in one
dependent family, under the supervision of one
" Bishop" of souls.

All the bishops of the Church on earth are limited
within specified districts, and sometimes restricted
to particular congregations ; but the " Bishop of
Souls " extends His superintending grace over all
lands. A converted man in China, and a Christian
in England, are equally near to their ever-watchful
Saviour. The spiritual religion of the Gospel has no
central shrine, to which the nations must come to
find the Lord. The first dispensation had this mark
of its temporary character ; at Jerusalem only could
the great privileges of the system be realized.
Christianity calls not the sons of God to make long
pilgrimages to consecrated places. The divine
" Bishop " being everywhere, each heart can hear

* Col. i. 18.

His voice speaking, wherever it seeks the holy teaching.

Ordinary bishops may meet the people at special times, and can rarely know each individual; but the "Bishop of Souls," being ever present with the whole Church, and with every member at all seasons, it follows that each hour may be a time of consecration, every day marked by a confirmation. It is not easy, with the world sitting so close to us, to feel the real spiritual presence of our Lord; and yet great is our danger, extreme our loneliness of heart, until we can say, with the Jewish king, " Thou art with me."*

The various bishops of the Church militant soon pass away from the scenes of their most active labours; their people listen to other voices, and are aided by other counsellors. The " Bishop of Souls" has no succession. He who watched over the persecuted Christians of the first ages, blessing some in dungeons, and speaking peace to others at the stake, still presides over the household of faith. Are we disposed to wonder that the " Bishop" should be the same, while His people have passed through such varying scenes? He, when on earth, went through many changes; one day received with Hosannas, another with the cry, " Crucify Him." It may be His pleasure that the Church, His body, should, in this respect too, be like her Head. Remember, that wherever His people have gone the heavenly bishop has gone with them. No Chris-

* Ps. xxiii. 4.

tian walks alone, either on the road of joy or on the path of sorrow. Pray earnestly that our eyes may not be always "holden."*

Many bishops of the Church have fallen into error and misled multitudes; but the "Bishop of Souls" is the "light of the world," and none who have made His words their guide, have ever mistaken the path of life. Men want an infallible, ever-present, ever-accessible guide in matters of religion. Surely the Lord must be such. Infallible, for He is "the Truth;" ever-present, for He has solemnly declared, "I am with you alway;" ever accessible, for He is not only "the way" and "the door," but commands us to "come unto" Him. Do we, with all our heart, believe this? If so, we shall, day by day, understand more clearly, and realize more fully, that spiritual presence of the Saviour, by which He becomes to each one of us "The Bishop of our souls."

THE CAPTAIN OF SALVATION.

Heb. ii. 10.

The march of the Israelites from Egypt to Canaan was, in some respects, symbolical of the soul's journey from the land of spiritual servitude to everlasting liberty and joy in the City of God.

* Luke xxiv. 16.

But as the exodus of the one involved the people in a long series of conflicts, so the advance of the Christian host is a continual succession of fightings. Strange it seems to some that the souls of the good cannot rest in a holy calm, waiting in tranquillity till the moment comes for crossing the mystical Jordan. War is the motto of life ; a long battle, or an endless slavery is the alternative. Peace indeed is promised ; it was the bequest of Jesus to His church :* not, however, the repose of the conqueror, but rather the confidence of the obedient and disciplined soldier in the skill and watchfulness of his general. The whole church of God is one vast phalanx, in which every individual must be equipped in celestial armour, or fall desperately wounded on the field.†

As the Hebrew host was placed under the command of Joshua, who led the tribes over Jordan, so the spiritual army of the living God has a leader, whose title, " The Captain of Salvation," gives assurance of final victory. The word translated " Captain "‡ is in two places rendered by " Prince,"§ in another by " Author,"‖ and thus reminds the Christian that his great leader is a King, and also the Author of all the qualities which fit the spiritual soldiers for their momentous warfare. Joshua could not impart his own power to the hearts of his followers ; but the " Captain of Salvation " not only

---

* John xiv. 27. † Eph. vi. 13—17. ‡ 'Αρχηγός. § Acts iii. 15, and v. 31. ‖ Heb. xii. 2.

leads, but infuses His own might into the souls of
those He commands.

This wonderful Leader provides both weapons
and armour for His otherwise helpless host.   The
" breast-plate of righteousness," " the shield of
faith," " the helmet of salvation," and " the sword
of the spirit," are not found in any earthly armoury :
each warrior receives the whole as a free gift from
the divine Captain.

. That Mighty One who so mysteriously appeared
to Joshua near the walls of Jericho, and before
whom the leader of the Hebrew army bowed in
adoration, announced Himself as "the Captain of
the Lord's host."* Thus early, under the first
dispensation, did the great leader make Himself
known as the sole commander of His people in the
great war against principalities and powers. Under
the character of "a leader and commander " the
voice of ancient prophecy announced Him ;† and
one of the last prophetic visions shows the glorified
Saviour heading "the armies of heaven."‡

These representations remind all believers that
the church is, in the truest sense, a " militant"
body; that every Christian is under the strict
regimen of war ; that our dedication to Christ partakes of the strictness of a military vow, binding
us to the most absolute, the most unquestioning
submission to "The Captain of Salvation."   All
disobedience, therefore, to our Lord's commands,
is a mutiny against the heavenly leader. The very

* Josh. v. 13—15.   † Isaiah lv. 4.   ‡ Rev. xix. 14.

word sacrament,* signifying a soldier's promise to obey his general, reminds us of the peculiar strictness of our obligations to Christ. "No one ever inquires into the reasons of a Rajah's order; when he says ' Go,' it is done." Such was the remark of a native of Nepaul to a European traveller; and it sets forth the literal duty of every spiritual soldier to whom the orders of the great " Captain " may come. Should He say " Go," let it be done. If the Christian dare, in his folly, attempt to carry on the war according to his own views, disregarding the leader's plans, shameful surprisals from the ever-watchful hosts of darkness will inevitably befal him.

We are to remember for our encouragement that the " Captain " knows the exact nature of the conflict, and the peculiar perils of each soldier. The divine Commander has not only borne a part in the fight, having encountered and defeated the very leader of the Satanic army, but has been made " perfect through sufferings."† Every weapon employed against His humblest follower has been already tried against Him : take courage then ; your Commander knows your peril : march onwards just in the way He points out, and you are safe.

There is one most comforting thought for every soldier of Christ—that victory is certain for all who keep to their colours. The banner of the cross must be borne over many a hard-fought field, but there can

---

* *Sacramentum* denoted the military oath in the Roman armies.

† Heb. ii. 10.

be no final defeat for those who follow to the end the
"Captain of their Salvation." The whole army of the
faithful shall have a share in the everlasting
triumph. In other wars the survivors alone carry
the palm of victory, the best and the bravest being
often left in unhonoured graves. But in this great
conflict every faithful warrior shall wear a crown—
all who "have fought the good fight" shall have a
triumph.

Earth is waiting for that great celebration of the
last victory; the whole creation is expecting the
end of the long war,* when the multitudes of earth,
the desperately wicked spirits of darkness, and the
hosts of attending angels, shall be witnesses of
Satan's complete defeat, and of the entry of the
armies of the redeemed into the promised land,
under the " Captain of their Salvation."

The Advocate.

1 John ii. 1.

A man conscious of some great offence which
endangers reputation, fortune, and life, seldom
ventures to undertake his own defence. His peril
leads him to secure the aid of the most able counsel.
His friends second such efforts, and the prosecutor
commends his prudence.

* Rom. viii. 19.

All who accept the Scriptures as a revelation and warning from God, must admit that every soul of man is exposed to a charge far more terrible than the accusations of any human indictment. The crime is high treason against the King of kings, and the penalty is everlasting death. In the face of such a charge, all metaphysical speculations on the origin of evil are but insults to the criminal. He has offended, and his practical inquiry is, "How can I escape the punishment?" A sinner who sees the fearful evil of sin and its consequences, will naturally feel that the great work of life is to find a means of escape from such a woe. When this has been accomplished, he will enter with a righteous earnestness into all the business of life. Daily duties, however lowly, however lofty, will come to him as God's appointed task : the progress of science, the development of art, the teachings of history, and the great movements in the kingdoms of the world, may well interest him who is at peace with God. But the awakened spirit must *first* make its "calling and election sure."* To him who thus feels, and who knows he has "sinned against heaven,"† how blessed must be the words, "We have an Advocate with the Father, Jesus Christ the righteous."

But how does the heavenly Advocate clear the sinner ? The accused usually hopes that his defender will obtain for him a verdict of "not guilty," by showing that the evidence against him

* 2 Peter i. 10.   † Luke xv. 21.

is insufficient. The repentant soul has no such
hope—cherishes no such wish. To plead "not
guilty" is far from his thoughts. The evidence of
sin is overwhelming; the Advocate knows this; the
Judge sees it all. The offender confesses the crime,
and nevertheless is justified before hell, earth, and
heaven.* He not only escapes punishment, but is
counted righteous. Herein consists the peculiarity
of that deliverance which the Lord accomplishes as
our "Advocate." He pays the penalty Himself,
dies for His client, and thus frees the offender for
ever. Though He bore the title of "the righteous,"
He became a "sin-offering,"† that all who seek His
advocacy might live among the justified.

But who brings the charge against the souls of
men? The powerful, subtle, wicked spirits, who,
having been permitted to tempt, then accuse mankind. We need not pause to inquire why these
fallen beings endeavour to ruin men, the solemn fact
has been stated in a mode well fitted to rouse all
into a sense of peculiar peril.‡ If such beings are
our unpitying accusers, a mighty "Advocate" is
clearly necessary. Looking to Him, and seeing
that the cause of every Christian has been undertaken
by the eternal Son of God, we may triumphantly
exclaim with the Apostle, "Who is he that condemneth?" "It is Christ that died."§ If then we

---

* Rom. v. 1.   † 2 Cor. v. 21.

‡ The Greek name, Διάβολος, a *calumniator*, reminds us that the
evil spirit is "the accuser of the brethren"; and the Hebrew, Sātān,
an *enemy*, exhibits him as the greatest and special foe of man.

§ Rom. viii. 34.

have secured the protection of the Divine Intercessor, let us fear no more the bitterest accusations of the whole host of wicked angels. They may bring heavy charges now; in the hour of death; even at the Day of Judgment; there is one answer, " We have an Advocate with the Father." The charge brought by Satan is true, we are verily guilty, but the voice of " the well-beloved Son " silences the accuser.

The word rendered " Advocate "* in 1 John ii. 1, also signifies a "Comforter,"† and one of the gracious Lord's offices is to comfort those He defends. The loving words, " I will not leave you comfortless, I will come to you," were not intended for the men of the Apostolic age only. They are daily verified still; the Advocate is with the Father, but He is also present with every believing heart.

The ablest advocate is fallible, and the knowledge of this often perplexes the client; the disciple of Jesus may, nay must, have unlimited confidence in his heavenly Counsellor, in " whom are hid all the treasures of wisdom and knowledge." He knows the mind of the everlasting Father, and is perfectly acquainted with the whole system of the Divine law and government.

One excellence of our Advocate is, that He gives His aid freely, " without money and without price." It was the boast of the ancient Roman advocates that they took no rewards for their services. The vaunt was not strictly true, for the eloquent pleader always claimed the support and votes of those for

* παράκλητος.   † See John xiv. 16—26.; xv. 26; xvi. 7.

whom he argued. Numerous clients could thus reward their patron, by raising him to the highest honours of the state. All this is a contrast to the work of our "Advocate"; He gives honour to us; we come to Him utterly impoverished, beyond the power of language to express, and He instantly abounds "toward us in all wisdom and prudence."* One such Advocate is sufficient for all souls, and one only is provided. The highest angel, the brightest spirit among the just "made perfect," has no power for such a work. In vain do misguided sinners turn to the saints, imploring their advocacy. Could these holy ones utter their warnings, each ignorant devotee would surely hear the words, "See thou do it not."†

We need so glorious, so perfect an Advocate, not to persuade the Father to accept us, for He is as willing to bless, as the Son is ready to intercede. Had the Father not "loved the world," an Advocate would not have been provided. The Judge of all the earth must be just; the eternal laws have been broken, the repentant sinners plead guilty, and the mighty Advocate comes forward to secure, at the same time, the punishment of sin, and the justification of the sinner. We are familiar with these doctrines; so fatally familiar it may be, that some feel little or nothing of the mystery which attracts the attention of angels.‡ Common truths tell of infinite verities, but he who "hath ears to hear" alone receives the heavenly lesson.

* Eph. i. 8.   † Rev. xix. 10.   ‡ 1 Peter i. 12.

"If any man sin" let him not draw back in despair, or hush conscience by the opiates of scepticism, or sooth his backsliding heart by the ritualism of superstition, or give up the spiritual struggle in the repose of formalism; but let such a one again seek for mercy, remembering that he has "an Advocate with the Father, Jesus Christ the righteous."

THE FAITHFUL WITNESS.

Rev. i. 5.

How often in the affairs of this life, does a man's fortune and good name depend upon his ability to make some disputed matter clear to his fellow men. One statement from an undoubted authority would suffice. In such an emergency what searches are made after a trustworthy witness.

So it must have been in the important matters of the life everlasting, had we been left with such knowledge only as reason could have given. With what an intense longing would inquiring minds have peered into the thick gloom around. With what eagerness would every probable speculation have been received. How vague, nevertheless, all answers to the questionings of the perplexed heart, must have been. Shall we have a life after this? Whither shall we go? Shall we be liable to danger and trouble in that future state? Will death separate

us for ever from the body? How does God regard
us? What does He wish us to do? Such might
have been the questions proposed by some of the
more thoughtful sons of men. Who could have
answered? Natural theology cannot give a decisive
reply; the stars in their courses, and the ever varying
phenomena of the earth, are unable to furnish a
clear response.

But answers of a most assuring fulness have been
graciously given. The Father of lights has sent
upon the earth His own beloved Son, to be unto
men a "faithful witness" respecting the things of
God. His fitness for this work is perfect. Do we
wish to know something certain about the future
state of souls? He can tell us everything necessary,
for He knows all the mysteries of the invisible
world. He has existed there from all eternity, and
His teaching is therefore that of an eye-witness.*
Do we wish to know how the everlasting Father
regards mankind? The Son is an all-sufficient
witness, for He alone "hath seen the Father;"†
He is "in the Father,"‡ from whom He received a
glorious message for men.§ Every word therefore
of His heavenly testimony must be full of the highest
knowledge. Whether He speaks of the Father's care
and special providence,‖ of the resurrection of the
dead,¶ of the immediate entrance of believing souls
into paradise,** or gives His solemn attestation to
the truths of the Old Testament,†† we may assuredly

---

* John. iii. 11.   † John vi. 46.   ‡ John xiv. 11.   § John xvii. 8.
‖ Matt. x. 29.   ¶ John vi. 40.   ** Luke xxiii. 43. †† John v. 39.

trust, with a peculiar confidence, in the declaration of such a " Witness."

The life of our blessed Lord was throughout its whole course, a succession of witnessings. The ignorant and prejudiced Jews endeavoured at certain times, to stop the utterance of the Lord's most important revelation;* the irritated and proud priests commissioned their officers to stop the divine testimony vouchsafed to their land.† Herod and his soldiery mocked the greatest Prophet earth should ever behold;‡ but amidst all this fierce striving of His creatures, the " faithful Witness " spoke the message of life. This characteristic of our Saviour's ministry was revealed to the ancient prophets, one of whom called the Jewish people to contemplate their future Messiah, as " a witness to the people."§

Jesus did not shrink from becoming a martyr-witness, being in this peculiar sense, the forerunner of that "noble army," which has in different ages and countries borne testimony to the Gospel, in the dungeon, on the rack, or at the fiery stake. What a comment on human blindness is the ever memorable fact, that the only divine "Witness" to men should have been martyred by men, The Lord foresaw His propitiatory and witnessing death from the beginning; none of His martyr followers had their final agony thus set continually before them. Our great Teacher was therefore a " faithful Witness " in a sense far above the most exalted of His disci-

* John viii. 58, 59. † John vii. 45, 46. ‡ Luke xxiii. 11. § Isa. lv. 4

ples : He having in this, as "in all things," the pre-eminence.

As Satan, at certain times, was permitted to approach the very throne of God,* so false witnesses were allowed to assail the Lord of truth.† Here indeed is a mystery of iniquity, that He who testified of life everlasting, to a dying world, who was the only completely "faithful witness" earth had ever heard, should, just at the close of His wonderful course, be attacked by suborned liars, urged on by wicked judges. What misrepresentations of motives, what perversions may not the disciples expect, when such was the conduct to which the heavenly Master submitted.

The Lord is a "faithful witness" still. His words of wisdom and love are sounding in our ears, His witnessing spirit is speaking now. Ofttimes the holy monitor is heard whispering of heavenly mysteries, bringing close to the listening ear words of deep and divine significance. The book of inspiration, the written volume of His faithful words, is indeed complete, a sufficient guide till time shall be no more. But the merciful and gracious Lord knows our tendency to look at the letter of the truth only ; and He therefore comes as the "faithful witness" to our souls, training them to see and feel the deep meanings, and the spiritual lessons, of which, without His aid, our dull spirits might not be sensible. Let us bear in mind the solemn truth that each true Christian "hath the witness in himself."‡

* Job i. 6.   † Mark xiv. 55, 56.   ‡ 1 John v. 10.

Titles of our Lord

AS

THE MEANS OF ACCESS TO THE FATHER.

The Door.
The Way.
The Forerunner.

THREE descriptive names lead our thoughts to Him who has "opened the kingdom of heaven to all believers." As *The Door*, we see in Him the only entrance to the Church militant and the Church triumphant. As *The Way*, we are reminded how close the road to the "many mansions" passes by the Cross; and as *The Forerunner*, we feel that His entrance to the "Father's House" has secured our admission there.

THE DOOR.

John x. 7, 9.

How do men enter into the true Church militant on earth ? The Lord of the spiritual fold Himself gives the clear and decisive answer, "I am the Door." The great Head of the " one family " knows exactly the manner in which each converted soul enters the household of faith ; and by applying to Himself this title, " The Door," He teaches us a vital truth. The question is not how men become members of the *visible* Church ; many sit within its enclosure who have never passed through Christ, " the Door." The sheep go into their own fold by the appointed way, but wolves may find or make other openings. How did *you* enter the Church ? The answer to this question will certainly show whether a man is to rank as a citizen of the city of God, or as a mere stranger, making a short stay within its walls.

How do souls enter the Church Triumphant ? Again the same answer will be given, " I am the Door." Thus all the blessedness of the regenerate on earth, all the glory of the redeemed in heaven, are reached through the one door.

So it always was. " I am the Door," was as true under the old dispensation as under the new. Did Abraham, who saw from afar the day of Christ, expect to enter into rest, save through Him ? However imperfect the knowledge of the patriarchs may have been, when compared with our light, their faith in early revelations could have directed them to no other "door." The formalist under the Mosaic dispensation, would, of course, regard the Levitical ceremonies as "The Door"; but the spiritually-minded Jews evidently trusted in Him to whom all the types pointed.

Many may have passed from earth into heaven in the times before the flood; multitudes probably ascended to their holy homes before the Lord appeared in human nature on the earth; a vast army of the redeemed will enter the holy city before the words, "time shall be no longer," are heard; but each one of that bright host will have gone into the eternal home through the same consecrated "Door."

One false religion* teaches that "fasting will carry a man to the gate of heaven, but almsgiving will open it." This is the spirit of all earthly systems; they tell man to seek heaven by certain fancied good works. Our all-wise Lord, who knows the exact value of human righteousness, bids us look to Him as the entrance.

Even now there are numerous guide-posts on life's road, which point in all directions, except to Christ "The Door." The delusive words, "This is the gate of heaven," stand near many a winding path, and those who disregard the direction of the divine finger, press on in multitudes.

* The Mahommedan.

Some come close to "The Door," but cannot
enter, because seeking to pass through with a
cumbrous load of superstitions.   Others wish to
pass with all the splendour of a sensuous and
artistic religion; and many will not enter unless
they can be followed by a long array of the pomps
and vanities of this world.   They then exclaim
against the narrowness of "The Door," which is,
nevertheless, wide enough for a whole world of
believing souls.

Thus the great multitude of the saved, though
they come from many lands, various ages, and even
various visible churches, are all made one in Him
who declares, "I am the Door."

The Way.

John xiv. 6.

The inhabitants of a modern civilized country
can form but a faint notion of those regions where
the most frequented ways were mere tracks made
by the traveller's foot: where the mountain torrent
rushed across the path, and the ravine or precipice
tried the courage of the wayfarer, and the strength
of his staff.   Such uncertain and perilous routes
are no unapt symbols of human religions—the ways
of the soul—which man had gradually formed for
himself.   They often began at some home of falsehood, crossed bleak and savage deserts, and ended

in a city of destruction. Even the Roman roads, which have endured the wear and tear of a thousand years, are but the representations of the more intellectual ways of error, along which whole nations marched. The world had lost its way, and seemed very unlikely to regain the right road. The multitude walked on, each believing his road the safe one; the philosophers, with a little more thought, argued about the different ways, and ended in perplexity. Statesmen advised each nation to walk contented in its own ancient road. Yet the world was dissatisfied; a feeling of suspicion crept over men, who wondered where the true road could be.

One voice, and one only, answered the question of the waiting earth. Jesus, who knew how far man had wandered, declared Himself to be "The Way." Prophets had long pointed to this "way," and foretold the approach of a time when all nations should walk in it.* But the way was essentially "new";† not one of the old human roads made straighter, or firmer, or of better materials. So fully was it fitted to conduct man into the land of delight, that one great man called it a "living way,"‡ and he was then walking in it, after having tried another road. But though new to the vast majority of mankind, it was, nevertheless, an *ancient* way, having been marked out for man immediately after he had lost his original home of blessedness. The great and good of olden times

* Isaiah xlii. 16.　　† Heb. x. 20.　　‡ Ib.

all walked along this road, and found the city of
God at the end.   It has also the peculiar characteristic of being the only way ever laid down from
earth to heaven.   Some expensively constructed
roads seem indeed, for a little way, to run in the
right direction, but all gradually turn off into the
deserts.   This way has also been "consecrated"*
for mankind, and that too by the one only High
Priest, who sprinkled it with His own most precious
blood.   Yet with all these wonderful peculiarities,
it is a *narrow* way,† being beset at the entrance by
many difficulties.   This is said of the way that
"leadeth unto life," and must, therefore, apply to
this new, living, ancient, only, and consecrated
way.   Nevertheless it has always been found wide
enough for the "multitude of the saved."

It is a royal way, for the "King of kings" has
in the words, "I am the Way," bestowed upon it
His own holy name.   Not only has a king thus distinguished this road, but it is further remarkable as
being used by none but kings,‡ for such is the rank
of all who walk therein.

That we may see more clearly the pre-eminent
excellence of "The Way," let us note to what it
infallibly leads every traveller.

Man having lost the sense of God's presence,
and being thus, in the language of Scripture,
"without God," must be recovered from this
atheism of the heart, which is far more difficult to
correct than the atheism of the head.   Now our

* Heb. x. 20.   † Matt. vii. 14.   ‡ Rev. i. 6.

Lord says that He alone is "The Way" to the Father:
" no man cometh unto the Father but by me,"* are
the words in which this most important doctrine is
stated. Whenever a regenerate soul finds God, it
finds Him in Christ. Is a great reconciliation being
accomplished ? it is "God in Christ" reconciling the
world unto Himself.† Men may discover God in
the movements of the heavens, in the laws of
vegetable life, in the mysteries of animal physiology,
and in the history of nations; but in this case
science is the way, not Christ; and such men are
often found to be in the Scripture view " without
God." A certain sentimentality often produces
poetic impressions of the Creator; and the understanding may see the marks of the divine hand in
the universe, and yet the heart never bend in
repentance as guilty, never rise in faith as pardoned.
The fallen angels themselves are not without very
strong feelings of the divine majesty, which moves
them even to trembling.‡ But they who approach
the eternal God by " The Way" opened through the
work of the Son, see Him as one who has pardoned,
is blessing, strengthening, and receiving them as
sons in Christ.

Our Lord is " The Way" *to peace*. The most
startling phenomena of human history are its wars.
The sword, the spear, and the battle-flag are seen
everywhere. The poor abound, living in wretched
homes and on bad food ; money would build better
houses, and provide many means of social elevation,

* John xiv. 6.　　† 2 Cor. v. 19.　　‡ James ii. 19.

but enormous funds are drawn off to construct
huge war ships. The people of many districts are
ignorant and debased; money would provide books
and the whole machinery of education; but millions
are required for floating batteries and impregnable
forts. The heathen are yet the majority of mankind; money would erect new missionary stations,
and increase the efficiency of the old; but hundreds
of thousands are spent in experimenting on cannon,
shot, and shell. What keeps society in this condition? The Gospel points to peace; and the Church
of Christ is, by her very constitution, a great peace
society. But war rages because the world has not
yet adopted the Saviour's doctrines and rules of
life. It has been said that society could not exist
if based on pure Gospel principles. Such an assertion is made without evidence, as society has never
yet received the laws of Christ for its guide.
Therefore to it the Lord has not been " The Way "
to peace.

Our Saviour is " The Way" to *happiness*. Some
say this has never been found on the earth. The
world is constantly planting the trees of joy, much
blossom appears, the fruit often reaches a certain
stage of growth, but not one in the course of six
thousand years has ever reached perfection. There
is some terrible defect in the climate or the soil of
the world. Yet the tree of happiness did once
grow upon the earth, flourishing awhile in Eden.
Will it ever grow again? Bright prophecies seem
to answer, Yes; but happiness will come through

Christ only, as "The Way." When man has tried
every other road; when moral, political, and social
organizations have failed to make humanity happy,
the wearied nations may listen to the heavenly
direction, " This is the way, walk ye in it."* But,
in the meantime, let each individual Christian see
that he fails not to obtain all the good which,
even here, the Saviour is ready to bestow. If
believers in Christ become false to their principles
by seeking any kind of blessing through other
means than "The Way," they, like the world, will
be miserably disappointed.

Is *perfection* a great object of desire to all
thoughtful hearts; to all who mourn over the
dimmed brightness of the world, once declared to
be "very good,"† and who look forward with joy
to the day when the whole church shall be glorious
and without blemish?‡ The world may hope for
perfection in certain sciences and mechanical arts,
though even in these new discoveries are continually
showing how little we have yet accomplished. But
how shall man himself be made perfect? Consider
what this involves: the body without weakness;
the mind without error; the will completely subject
to God; the best ends ever aimed at; the best
means always chosen; peace universal; knowledge
deep, pure, and increasing; all the mental faculties
strong and working rightly; all the feelings heavenly,
and the whole soul absorbed in the love and service
of God in Christ. Is this really promised? Our

* Isaiah xxx. 21. † Gen. i. 31. ‡ Eph. v. 27.

Lord is "The Way" to this perfection; every Christian shall become "perfect," and attain even to "the stature of the fulness of Christ."* Look upwards, then, towards the coming glories; perfection is attainable; man's ruined nature shall be completely restored; a period brighter than the far-famed golden age is coming; but all this unspeakable fulness of joy is to be obtained through Him alone who is "The Way."

THE FORERUNNER.

Heb. vi. 20.

When the Jewish high priest entered the holy of holies on the day of atonement, not one of the worshipping multitude expected to follow him into the mysterious inner sanctuary. They knew that the ark was there; they were confident that the priest would sprinkle the blood before the mercy-seat, and that the incense would rise up before the cherubim. But the desire of entering the hidden sanctuary would have been checked as sinful by the devout Israelites. They could never regard the high priest as their "forerunner," for none expected to enter within the veil. In this respect there is an instructive contrast between the high priest of the law and Jesus, who is in every sense "The Forerunner" of all believers. The Lord has entered into the holy of holies, and the whole church of God shall follow in the appointed time.

* Eph. iv. 13.

The Jewish priest entered for his own nation only; but Jesus has gone into the heavens as "The Forerunner" of a multitude of all tribes and people from many a distant region, of which the sons of Aaron never heard. Such contrasts show us the comprehensiveness of the new dispensation when compared with the old. The one tended to separate the Jew from the nations, the other trains the Christian to regard all men as brethren, since for men of all people the Redeemer has ascended into heaven as " The Forerunner."

The Apostle is careful to remind us of the great object of our Saviour's entrance into the holiest; He is there " for us." We need to be reminded that the Lord of Glory is working and acting for His people *now*, without intermission. Who cares for us? may sometimes be the querulous inquiry of men who have not yet learned to regard Christ in His kingly and priestly characters. The Christian, unless faith be weak, has no such disquieting fears, knowing that His Lord is ruling all things by the word of His power. As the high priest did not forget, in the solemn solitude of the inmost· sanctuary, his waiting countrymen who were kneeling outside the veil, so our " Forerunner" has in His heart the dearest interests and well-being of His people on earth. We know what the high priest did when he stood in the holy of holies, and we are not left in ignorance of that glorious work in which the Lord is now engaged. As the blood of the sin-offering was sprinkled before the ark, which con-

tained the tables of the broken law, and before the
mercy-seat, to remind all that forgiveness comes
through sacrifice, so our Forerunner has borne into
the "Holy Place" the unspeakable efficacy of "His
own blood,"* sufficient to satisfy infinite justice,
while it procures infinite mercy. The priest also
carried within the veil a peculiar and precious
incense;† and we may see, in the heavenly vision,
that incense was offered "with the prayers of all
saints."‡ We know that our petitions are to go up
before the Father in the name of Jesus;§ and this
incense offered in the Jewish sanctuary reminds us
of the intercession of our Lord for us, through
which the rich blessings of redemption descend on
the waiting church.

Our "Forerunner," Jesus, has entered heaven to
prepare a holy place for us;‖ a work altogether
distinct from any rite belonging to the office of the
Jewish high priest. In what this preparation of the
heavens for the redeemed consists we know not,
but are well assured that "the holy City, new
Jerusalem," will have in it "the glory of God," and
the "light" of the Lamb.¶

As on the day of atonement but one priest
entered within the veil, so there is but one "Forerunner for us." Multitudes have long ago passed
into the Holy Place of renewed souls ; all these are,

---

* Heb. ix. 12.

† This incense is said to have been a compound of stacte, onycha,
galbanum, and frankincense.

‡ Rev. viii. 3.   § John xv. 16.   ‖ John xiv. 2.   ¶ Rev. xxi. 2, 11, 23.

in a chronological sense, our forerunners—they enter before us, but not "for us." In like manner the spirits of the redeemed who are now being summoned to their rest may be called the forerunners of all who shall follow them.

But "for us" Christ alone has entered; no prophet, apostle, martyr, or saint, can or would share in that honour. As the Lord alone came down from heaven "for us," lived on earth "for us," died "for us," and rose "for us," so He alone has returned to His glory as "The Forerunner for us."

When the Jewish priest had passed within the veil, he was completely separated from the worshippers without; this is not the case with the church and her Lord. She indeed sees Him not, the veil being between; but He, by His divine power, is still present with every believing heart. As our "Forerunner" He may seem far away; but He really is so near, that He liveth in us.*

If, then, we are now looking to Him as our "Forerunner," we must regard ourselves as His followers; keeping in His road, doing His work, receiving His spirit, and trusting solely in His mediation. If thus we are enabled to follow Him, soon, very soon, the veil of mystery will be opened; we shall pass into the Holy of Holies, to realize the triumph both of mercy and justice, and be presented "without spot" before the Father by our one glorious "Forerunner."

* Gal. ii. 20.

Titles of our Lord

as

THE SOURCE OF LIFE.

THE RESURRECTION.
THE FIRST-BORN FROM THE DEAD.
THE LIFE.

THESE three deeply significant titles lead us to exclaim, "O grave, where is thy victory?" In *The Resurrection,* and in *The First Born from the Dead,* we behold the final conqueror of death; and as *The Life,* we know that because He liveth we shall live also.

THE RESURRECTION.

John xi. 25.

The ancient Greek philosophers regarded the body as the enemy of the soul. Being ignorant of the true cause of sin, they ascribed it to the influence of matter upon the mind. The latter was spoken of as dwelling in a prison-house of flesh, and the day of liberation from a material home was deemed the hour of freedom. To such men the doctrine of the resurrection brought no satisfaction; and Athens mocked when the Apostle preached "the resurrection of the dead."* So widely spread was this delusion, that even some of the early and less stable Christians were caught by the snare, saying, "There is no resurrection of the dead,"† or that the "resurrection is passed already."‡ Some few were so completely enslaved by heathen notions of the sinfulness of matter, that they even denied the reality of the Lord's body, and therefore His humanity. To such the Apostle probably refers when speaking of some who did not confess that Jesus Christ "had come in the flesh."§

In opposition to all these errors, the Gospel proclaims a rising from the dead; and our Redeemer draws men to Himself by the emphatic words, "I am the Resurrection." All the believing hearts

* Acts xvii. 32. † 1 Cor. xv. 12. ‡ 2 Tim. ii. 18. § 2 John v. 7.

among the Jews had long received the doctrine;
and even in the ancient patriarchal times the same
truth exalted the faith of the world's fathers.* But
when the Lord of Glory proclaimed Himself to the
bereaved sister as "The Resurrection," a brighter
ray of hope rested henceforth on every believer's
grave.   Christ, as "The Resurrection," first broke
the fetters of the tomb, and triumphed over a foe
unvanquished till that moment. Man might well
imagine the ruin to be irreparable, when he saw the
body laid in the grave, and the deep quietude of
that mysterious rest remain age after age unbroken.
The conquerors who had shaken earth, whose very
names had been watchwords of victory, were all
lying "each in his narrow cell." The countless
multitudes of many generations also seemed for
ever laid low, like the fallen leaves of autumn.
And there came a day when He, who had raised
human hope by the words, "I am the Resurrection,"
Himself was borne into one of those silent homes
of the dead. All might well seem over then; and
the strange solemn darkness, which had gathered
round the cross, appeared typical of the gloom
coming over the earth. But a morning came when
that garden-tomb was empty. "The Resurrection" had become a fact; the risen Lord had been
seen. Not even the iron rule of Roman military
discipline could keep the affrighted soldiers to
their post; and the Jewish priests, who would
gladly have exposed to view the body of Jesus had

* Job xix. 26.

He not risen, tried to hide their defeat by a lie, which bore folly and fraud in its front. Thus had the Lord gloriously proved Himself to be " The Resurrection." That sacred body which rose from the tomb above eighteen hundred years ago, is at this moment on the throne, though hidden from our view, and will one day be made visible to all nations. We may hope to see many wonderful things, but this manifestation of Christ's glorified body we are certain to witness.

This title, " The Resurrection," brings the Lord before us as the great restorer of our bodies from the grave. Had He not risen, the earth would have held all her dead within her prison-houses for ever. How the scattered particles, not of one body, but of all bodies, can be brought together, is a question which must be left to His decision who is " The Resurrection." Even in our present state there are many significant instances of the wonderful combinations into which matter may be forced by the divine agency, which on each returning spring combines a few gases and simple elements into all the rich variety of floral beauty. When we walk by the quiet graves of Christian friends, let us remember that He who is " The Resurrection " has secured by His own rising the restoration of all those buried ones.

He will thus abolish death; for where will the king of terrors have a single trophy when every human body, from that of Adam to the last man, shall have been raised from the grave ? The Lord will, by this means, complete the happiness of the redeemed, when the bodies and souls of all who "sleep in Jesus" shall be eternally re-united, after a separation for centuries, and even thousands of years. Each Christian, save those who may be alive at the coming of the Lord,* will taste the mysterious bitterness of death, but each shall also experience the exceeding joy of the re-union of body and soul.

What manner of life is reserved for the raised bodies of the saints is among the things not revealed; but if we should reverently ask, "with what body do they come?"† five short answers have been graciously given by the Lord, through His Apostle St. Paul. To receive these intimations thankfully is our duty; to speculate rashly upon them will be our folly.

We are told that Christ will fashion the bodies of His saints "like unto His glorious body."‡ This short statement justifies us in humbly entertaining the loftiest expectations respecting the future body. "Like unto His," opens out before us the grandest views. These time-worn tenements of clay, "battered and decayed," broken by diseases, crushed by permitted accidents, utterly dissolved at last in the retreat of the grave, are, nevertheless, to become "like unto His glorious body." Let us then no longer speak of *death*, let us call it the Christian's sleep.

The same Apostle gives four revelations in one

---

* 1 Cor xv. 51.   † 1 Cor. xv. 35.   ‡ Phil. iii. 21.

chapter respecting the raised bodies of believers. He tells us they shall possess "incorruption,"* an idea we are unable to grasp, so utterly remote is it from the law of the present life. Here all is change, and the change is that of corruption. Our bodies are dying every moment—parting with some portion of their substance; and death is stayed only so long as new matter can be assimilated to the system. Scientific men tell us that every man who reaches the age of fifty has outlived the matter of four or five successive bodies. Such is the rate of decay on earth. But all this will be changed after the resurrection, for the body shall be raised in "incorruption" by the power of Him who is "The Resurrection."

It is also to be raised "in glory"; this will present a wonderful contrast to the dishonour now done to the body. Could we see at one glance all the sufferings and humiliations endured by the bodies of men throughout the world in the course of one day only, we should hail with a holy fervour of joy the announcement that all this shall be rectified by a rising "in glory." Our loving Saviour has determined that the redemption of the body shall be as complete as the salvation of the soul.

This tabernacle "in which we groan" shall be raised "in power,"† and thus fitted to co-operate with the soul in all the matters of the heavenly life. In this world the noblest purposes and well-designed plans come to nought, because the body

* 1 Cor. xv 42.   † 1 Cor. xv. 43.

fails in the great conflict.   But when the spirit
shall be "perfect," and the body "in power," all
service will be easy, and all work joy.

The Lord, as "The Resurrection," has also
ordained that the body of every one who sleeps in
Him shall be spiritual.   Human language fails to
convey the full idea of the refinement, exaltation,
and fitness of the heavenly life which such a term
suggests.

Our risen Lord having secured for our bodies
such honour, and having proclaimed Himself as
"The Resurrection," let us use these tabernacles
for His glory only; let us shrink no more at the
sight of the grave, which is but the safe place of
rest where the Saviour keeps His holy ones.   He is
surely coming; the day of wonders is approaching,
when He shall call the heavens from above and the
earth from beneath to behold the victory over death
and the grave won by Himself alone, as "The
Resurrection."

The First-born from the Dead.

Col. i. 18. Rev. i. 5.

When Lazarus was called from the tomb by the
voice of Jesus, the spectators gazed upon their
restored friend with a wondering awe.   Next to the
Lord, the brother of Mary and Martha must have
been the most observed of all the guests at that

supper in Bethany, where he sat at the table with
Him* who was the "Resurrection and the Life."
Two such guests had never, since the world began,
sat together until that hour. Yet Lazarus was not
the complete freedman of the tomb. For a few
days or years he walked on the earth, to show forth
the glory of his Lord; and then there came another
day of death and another burial: Lazarus "sleepeth"
still, as to his body, and will sleep on until "the
dead shall hear the voice of the Son of God."†
Great was the honour granted to such as Lazarus;
the restoration was, however, but a respite. Not
one of these could be called "begotten from the
dead," for to the dead all returned again.

There standeth One visible to the eye of faith,
who is not only "begotten from the dead," a privilege in which all will have a share, but is "The
First-begotten from the dead." He entered the
grave no more; to His first entombment He submitted for us, but there came no second burial for
the Prince of Life. Thus in the order of rising
from the grave our ever-blessed Lord has a glorious
pre-eminence. He alone is "The First-begotten of
the dead." Had one among the saints been finally
rescued before the rising of the Saviour, this title
could not have been His. In the hour of His last
mysterious agony "the graves were opened"; but
though many a rock tomb was then rent, not one of
the sleepers rose "until after the resurrection."‡

As the Saviour is "The *First*-begotten from the

* John xii. 2, 9.   † John v. 25.   ‡ Matt. xxvii. 52, 53.

dead," there is coming a second day of triumph, in
which all His ransomed ones shall have a share. To
one death and one burial the loving and mighty Lord
submitted for us; one death and one dissolution of
the body all, save a few at the last,* must undergo.
But, in the appointed time, there shall come the
hour when *all* shall be "begotten from the dead."
The bodies of men will then receive that second
life, which, unlike the temporary resurrection of
Lazarus, will be enduring. Some may, indeed,
"wake to shame"† and contempt, but to the dust
they shall no more return after such a waking.
Does the time seem long since "The First-begotten
from the dead" rose to the heavens? Does the
delay amaze? Consider awhile the standard by
which the chronology of Heaven is reckoned—"one
day is with the Lord as a thousand years, and a
thousand years as one day."‡ This spiritual calcu-
lation, perplexing as it may appear to us, was
adopted by the church under the old dispensation,§ and is emphatically enforced upon us in the
cautionary words, "Be not ignorant of this."

But while the church is waiting for the redemption of the body ‖—for the hour when "The First-
begotten from the dead" shall fulfil His promise,
"I will come again"¶—let us watch for the signs
of the times which indicate to thoughtful and believing hearts the gradual and certain approach of
the Lord.

* 1 Cor. xv. 51.   ‡ 2 Peter iii. 8.   ‖ Rom. viii. 23.
† Dan. xii. 2.   § Psalm xc. 4.   ¶ John xiv. 3.

The glorified body of the Saviour, which, as the first-fruits of the resurrection, is now hidden from our view in the light which no man can approach unto,"* shall yet be seen by every eye. When "The First-begotten from the dead" rose early on that memorable "first day of the week," the attending angels and the terrified Roman soldiers alone beheld this first great victory won by Jesus for His people. But when He shall come to manifest Himself to the world as "The First-begotten from the dead," far different will be the host of adoring or wondering beholders. The angels will be there† to join in the triumphs of Him who is the Head of all their "principalities and powers." All the kindreds of the earth, every nation and tongue, the men of the antediluvian and the patriarchal times shall be there, as witnesses of Christ's complete victory over the grave.

Great, even to an awful degree, will be the differences in that vast gathering of the lost and the saved. But all will agree in witnessing that "The First-begotten from the Dead" will then have completed His glorious work. How strange the earth will seem when not one grave retains its long-imprisoned occupant! The secret tombs of the pyramids shall be opened, and the deep caverns and sands of ocean must give up the dead. Will the hymn, "O grave, where is thy victory? O death, where is thy sting?" be sung on that day of triumph?

* 1 Tim. vi. 16.   † Matt. xxv. 31.

Let us, then, commit the bodies of Christians to
the earth as to a consecrated sleeping-place, from
which, after their appointed rest, they shall all come
forth as the trophies and the witnesses of His
glory who is " The First-begotten from the dead."

THE LIFE.

John xi. 25.   Col. iii. 4.   1 John i. 2.   1 John v. 12.

Men who fear nothing else, fear death ; even the
bravest spirits are often the veriest cowards in the
presence of this foe. The feelings of the whole
human race, are expressed in the comprehensive
language of the patriarch, who called death " the
king of terrors."* To delay the approach of this
dreaded visitation, men have sacrificed riches,
honours, truth, friends, country, and religion. He
then who can deliver from death will surely have
the world at His feet. Is there such a mighty one ?
Our glorious Lord answers the question, proclaiming
Himself " The Life." He does not indeed immediately destroy the grave, but He makes it the gate
to life. Listen to the sublime declaration first made
by the Saviour, near a Jewish burial ground, and
now repeated hourly in the ear of faith, " Whosoever
liveth and believeth in Me shall never die." Then
came the searching question, "Believeth thou this ?"

* Job xviii. 14.

Let us then realize with exulting hearts, the fact that, "The Life" has come into this world of death, promising a resurrection for the body, and a quickening for the soul.

In one very peculiar sense Christ is "The Life"; all forms of existence, visible and invisible, having come from Him as from an infinite fountain of being.* Where now the starry universe lights up the immeasurable depths of space, there was once a total blank. That void was filled by the creative Word, who now stands ready to pour spiritual life into each heart. Some men, in our age, deny the possibility of miracles; do they admit a creation? If so, that surely is a miracle, and was wrought by Him who is "The Life" of all things. The many mansions in the Father's house are now inhabited by a bright host of spirits "made perfect," and each of these has received both his natural and regenerate nature from "The Life." Every Christian on earth has also within him a mysterious and vital energy, "hid with Christ,"† as the fountain whence it rose. Thus the whole creation, the redeemed in heaven and the redeemed on earth, can trace their varied forms of life to Him, by whom "all things consist."‡

The rich outpouring of heavenly gifts from this fountain of "Life," is characterized by its perfect *freeness*. Man did not procure his own creation, neither does he purchase his own salvation. Every good and every perfect gift "cometh"§ to men,

---

* John i. 3.; Col. i. 16.   † Col. iii. 3.   ‡ Col. i. 17.
§ James i. 17.

and is not bought; yet there is a feeling in the
heart, prompting us to *earn* the divine gifts, to
deserve them by some merit of ours. Life in the
creature may be originated by the direct agency of
God, as when the world came into being at the
heavenly word, or when Saul of Tarsus received the
holy call from above, without the intervention of any
visible means. Or life may be the result of certain
natural or spiritual laws; as the harvest of this year
has sprung from seed sown; or, as the turning of a
mind from darkness to light, may be traced to the
reading of a book, or the occurrence of some impressive incident. But in each case the gift was free.

As "The Life," Christ *sustains* existence, being
not only the life giver, but the life supporter. There
is no self-upholding power in the creature, whose
energies would soon pass away, unless ever renewed
from some higher source, as the stream must dis-
appear if the spring were to cease. The planetary
bodies are kept in their orbits by mysterious forces
acting every moment, and all the living souls in the
purchased Church of Christ, are sustained in their
spiritual movements by the influence of Him who is
their "Life." Emphatic indeed is that declaration
of the Apostle, in which he acknowledges the
absolute dependence of his whole spiritual being on
his Saviour; "I live, yet not I, but Christ liveth in
me."* This experience is not peculiar to apostles,
or to apostolic times, but is true of every believer in
every age.

* Gal. ii. 20.

" The Life was manifested and we have seen it,"* are the words of one who was a chosen associate of the Lord. Is " The Life " ever manifested now ? Yes ; but only those see the glorious presence, who live under the solemn and abiding sense of things invisible. Christ has not left His Church, He is in the midst of her, guiding her through all the complications of earth, and guarding her against the subtle counsels of " the gates of hell."† His working and His presence are, of course, hidden from those who believe in the visible only. As they see not God manifesting His wisdom, in the wonderful structure of a spring flower, or in the beautifully adapted mechanism of animal bodies, so they see not Christ controuling the strangely complex human world. " The Life " is wondrously close to us, let all recognize, each in his own little but important daily world of thought and action, the present Lord. Many have gained this spiritual vision ; the result of great manifestations of Christ in critical times—some had almost made shipwreck of faith, even the world could see the rocks a-head, and the gathering storm, but the backsliding Christian saw no peril. A moment came when the far-distant lighthouse of hope was hidden, and ruin seemed at hand. But then, when no lifeboat of human help was near, the Lord shewed Himself, walking over a sea of trouble, hushing the storm, and bringing into a safe harbour the weak disciples. Well may such rescued ones feel how near " The Life " is to His people.

* John i. 2. † Mat. xvi. 18.

He is needed now; He will be needed for ever.
Myriads of ages will pass away, and we be in far
exalted heavenly mansions, the whole system of the
universe may have changed, and higher modes of
being, which no human heart had imagined, may
become familiar to us; but all this eternal fulness
of delight will flow from Him who is now and ever
will be, " The Life " of the redeemed.

---◆---

Titles of our Lord

AS

THE CAUSE OF UNION AND STRENGTH.

---◆---

THE TRUE VINE.
THE CHIEF CORNER-STONE.
THE HEAD OF THE CHURCH.

THESE names of the Saviour point out the nature
and cause of oneness. How clearly does *The True
Vine* represent Him as the centre from whom every
spiritual branch draws its life, and by whom each is
connected with all. As *The Chief Corner-stone* the
Lord appears giving both oneness and strength to

the " House of God "; and as *Head of the Church*
we see the mysterious relationship subsisting between
all regenerate souls and their ever-living Head.

THE TRUE VINE.

John xv. 1.

A great writer tells us there are "sermons in
stones "; and does not the Christian see God his
Father, and Christ his Saviour, in all things? To
the ear of faith every object in nature speaks. The
vivid richness of spring, the sombre grandeur of
autumn, the "cold sublimity" of lofty mountains,
and the expanse of ocean, have often suggested to
irreligious but poetic minds thoughts full of beauty.
But to a believer the visible universe presents anal-
ogies and images more glorious, and utters words of
deeper and more solemn significance than earthly
poet ever sung. Blessed are they who have thus
learned to find Christ everywhere. To them the
world is · full of a heavenly music, each note of
which awakens hallowing associations.

It is clearly the will of God that we should thus
use His works to remind us of His Son. The glories
of the eternal Word are represented to us by figures
drawn from nature. In one scripture the Saviour is
described as a " Sun of Righteousness,"* in another
as a " great light,"† as " a branch,"‡ as a " tender

* Mal. iv. 2.   † Isaiah ix. 2.   ‡ Isaiah xi. 1.

plant,"* and as "rivers of water."† The Lord
Himself adopted similar natural objects to set forth
His mediatorial character, when He called Himself
" the Light of the world," and described the mysterious union of the Church with her Head, in the
words, " I am the true Vine."

Probably, when these words were spoken, a vine
was within view of the disciples, perhaps growing in
the court of the house where the paschal supper was
celebrated. Thus their hearts would receive, through
both eye and ear, the holy lesson. But though the
presence of the natural vine, and that of Christ
Himself, may have quickened their apprehensions,
the doctrine contained in the symbol is as true and
important for us as for them. The vines of Palestine
may no longer enrich as of old, the once cultivated
hill-terraces, but eighteen centuries have not weak-
ened the beautiful significance of the words, " I am
the true Vine." Rather, as age succeeds age, the
Church sees more fully the fitness of this title.

" The Vine " undoubtedly reminds us of the *union*
subsisting between Christ and all His disciples. The
youngest and smallest shoot at the end of the longest
branch of a far-spreading vine, is as truly a part of
the tree as the oldest branch which proceeds direct
from the stem. So, the last and weakest convert
from heathenism is one with his redeeming Lord,
no less than the perfected spirit of an apostle or
martyr. It is difficult to realize this ; to feel that
the latest convert among the American Indians, or

---

* Isaiah liii. 2.   † Isaiah xxxii. 2.

P

the Esquimaux, is not only our brother, a point slowly admitted by some, but even the brother of Christ. This is no sentimental fiction or figure of speech, but one of those great truths which belong to the Gospel plan of redemption. This oneness is not to be described by negatives; but we may safely say, that it does not consist in uniformity of name. A whole nation may be called Christian, and one half be virtually heathen in principle and practice. Nor is the oneness that of a Church system only. There may be one liturgy in one language under one organization, and the whole society may move obedient to one well devised rule, and yet that Church may resemble a branch lying on the ground, having been cut off from "the Vine."

Where there is unity there will be *agreement.* No opposition exists between "the Vine" and the branches; there is no discord between Christ and His members. Visible churches may contend, creeds may be at variance, but between the Lord and His redeemed ones there will be a spiritual accord. We do not indeed always see this in matters of doctrine; Christ's people sometimes mistake their Master's orders, and misinterpret their Teacher's words. The agreement is in aims— Christ came to save men; every Christian is in some degree a worker with the Saviour in this great object. Christ loves the Church, and all who have "passed from death unto life,"* are drawn towards those who have received the same great atonement.

* 1 John iii. 14.

The unity denoted by the vine is not therefore a oneness between Christ and His Church only, but a most holy accord between all parts of the Church itself. Christians are beautifully described as one "family;"* and in the glorious unity the apostle includes not only the feeble, tempted, and struggling followers of Christ now on the earth, but all the triumphant and glorified souls in the heavenly mansions. In this respect the Church of Christ may truly be called "*semper eadem,*" (always the same) "the communion of saints" being independent of nationalities or languages. A true believer in the midst of England's metropolis will sympathize with a Christian in the solitude of an Alpine valley.

As the branches *resemble* the stem in all essential qualities, so Christ, "the true Vine," imparts to believers the transforming graces and heavenly gifts which change sinful men into "sons of God."† Herein we see the reality of the Spirit's regenerating work. Christians are not to aim after a likeness to even the greatest and noblest of mankind. Conformity "to the image" of the Son is the glorious object of the Gospel plan.‡ It is therefore a royal likeness, a divine pattern which is set before us.

We may note, with a rejoicing reverence and adoring gratitude, the various particulars of this resemblance. Is Christ holy? So must His people become§. Is He a Son? So are they through Him.‖ Is He an Heir? so are the meanest of His followers.¶

* Ephesians iii. 15.   ‡ Romans viii. 29.   ‖ Romans viii. 14.
† John i. 12.   § Ephesians v. 27.   ¶ Romans viii. 17.

Is He a King? such royal honour belongs to all believers.* Is the Lord a High Priest? all His disciples have been made "priests unto God."† Is He the Life? all who love Him have "passed from death."‡ Does "the fulness of the Godhead" dwell in Him? His redeemed ones are "the temple of God."§ Thus do believers bear in a high and glorious sense "the image of the heavenly."|| With how holy a care should all who possess this likeness keep their robes unspotted.

Our great Teacher calls Himself "the Vine," to teach us our complete *dependence* upon Him. The most flourishing branch, that which bore the richest fruit, perishes in a few hours when severed from the vine. Christ is "our life" in every sense. He begins, He continues, He perfects life. A solemn lesson for churches; a momentous truth for every Christian. "Without Me ye can do nothing,"¶ is a passage requiring no verbal commentary. The deep significance of those words has been illustrated in every age by many a sad spiritual ruin. History, that solemn witness for God, tells us of churches, which being for a period drawn away from Christ, substituted for His life-giving aid the props of a dry human learning and a cloudy philosophy. The props gave way, and the sound of approaching ruin warned some of those heedless churches back to their Lord. Others lie prostrate like storm-riven trunks. The glitter of a ceremonial worship may hide the

* Revelation i. 6.   ‡ 1 John iii. 14. || 1 Cor. xv. 49.
† Revelation i. 6.   § 1 Cor. iii. 16.   ¶ John xv. 5.

decline of a Christian society, but Christ can alone revive its life. True philosophy and true learning worship near the Cross, but they cannot be made substitutes for the grace that is in Christ Jesus.

The Lord, when He called Himself "the True Vine," reminded us of the heavenly *discipline* and divine training provided for His people. As the branches are not left to trail uselessly along the ground, or to waste their strength in a hurtful luxuriance of foliage, so the Father preserves, guides, and regulates the growth of all the plants in the spiritual vineyard.*

There are two classes of branches on the vine— the barren and the fruit-bearing; so there are two kinds of pruning, the total cutting away, and the tender careful training, which uses the knife to produce fruit. So in the visible Church a severance for destruction is daily going on; a discipline to life is hourly experienced. The history of the Church utters many a solemn lesson on this subject. Have not large portions of the vineyard been extirpated and left, for a season at least, to be waste? Not because there was no fruit, but the grapes had become "wild."† Where are the four hundred churches of North Africa? That part of the vineyard has been left to be trodden down. The Koran is read where Christ was preached. Yet there was a cause; corruption gradually entered, the truth as it is in Jesus was neglected; Christ was hidden and man exalted : then came the cutting east wind of the

* John xv. 2.   † Isaiah v. 4.

Mahommedan desolation. Well may other churches
watch lest a like ruin befall them.

To keep close to Christ, close to His pure and
heavenly Gospel, is our only safety. Let no human
system come, like a hedge of thorns, between the
Lord and us. To compromise with error, to con-
clude a truce with falsehood, is high treason against
our King. But the ear will soon cease to distinguish
the voice of Jesus if the heart lose its sense of oneness with Him, who lovingly and beautifully describes
Himself as "The True Vine."

THE CHIEF CORNER-STONE.

Eph. ii. 20.   1 Peter ii. 6.

The "laying the foundation stone" must have
been an important incident among all people. The
first stone of the great pyramid, or of the royal
palace at Nineveh, or the Roman Colosseum, was
doubtless laid amidst high expectations and solemn
ceremonials. Some of these foundation stones yet
support their massive superstructures. How time-
defying do the Pyramids seem ! how grandly stands
the Colosseum ! Yet the mark of decay is upon
them ; even the structures of the proud Pharoahs
are crumbling ; their long-hidden tombs have been
broken, and the bones of a pyramid builder are to
be seen in the British Museum.* So pass away the

* The body of King Menka-re, who is supposed to have built the
second pyramid, is preserved in a glass case in the Egyptian Room.

mightiest works of man; the ruins of empires
teaching him to renounce his vain dreams of an
earthly immortality.   Men, in their pride, may call
cities "eternal," and the works of human genius
may be designated "immortal," but slowly and
surely the "night of ages" hides the pomp and
glory of time.

There is, however, a building which shall for
ever stand — "the city of the living God, the
Heavenly Jerusalem,"* of which the Lord Jesus
declares, "that the gates of hell shall not prevail
against it."†   This is the only building which,
having its foundations laid on the earth, shall
endure for evermore.   But the cause of its duration
is clear — "its builder and maker is God,"‡ who
laid the corner-stone in the place foretold by His
prophet.§

This title, "Chief Corner-stone," reminds us of
the true foundation of the church, which stands,
and must for ever stand, on Christ alone.   Wisdom,
eloquence, and learning may suspend their tribu-
tary garlands on the walls, but not all the wise
systems of all the sages can add one stone to the
foundation of the Lord's house.   The apostles were
wise master builders; but one of their number
warned the infant church of his day, that "other
foundation" than Christ could not be laid.‖   The
history of Christianity is one continued comment
on this warning.   See what shocks the church has

* Heb. xii. 22 and 28.   † Matt. xvi. 18.   ‡ Heb. xi. 10.
§ Isa. xxviii. 16.   ‖ 1 Cor. iii., 11.

stood when built on Christ: see how the floods
have swept her works away when, in her folly, she
has built on the sands of men's doctrines. An
erring church may even build upon a rock, but if
the rock be cut from a quarry of the earth, the
superstructure, however imposing, will be brought
down in the day of tempests. The disciples pointed
with pride to the massive foundation stones of the
temple, but in a few years national corruption
turned that magnificent pile into a blackened ruin,
and now a Mahommedan mosque stands on the site.
Want of faith in a crucified Saviour, and reliance on
human works, will bring any church to desolation.

"The Corner-stone" suggests also that true
church *unity* can only be secured by building on
Christ. As the massive "corner-stone" united the
walls of a building, so the Lord by His heavenly influences brings into one all the various members of
the Christian family. The walls of an edifice may
be formed of different materials, and erected by
various builders, yet the corner-stone connects them.
So in the church Christ makes His people one, not
by mere outward uniformity, but by a true brother-
hood of heart. Many particulars of this unity might
be enumerated, but it may suffice to suggest that
all true members of Christ hold one atoning sacrifice, one imputed righteousness, one regeneration by
the operation of the Holy Spirit, one sanctification,
one great object to live according to the Lord's will,
and one grand hope "to be for ever with the Lord."
Christ as "The Corner-stone" thus links in hal-

lowing sympathies the whole multitude of the faithful, who have, in a high and spiritual sense, "all things in common."

This "Chief Corner-stone" is called "elect,"* not because of a selecting from amongst others, as Christians are chosen out of the mass of mankind, for the eternal Father had but one Son upon whom to lay the guilt of man. The epithet seems rather to denote that mysterious fore-ordaining "before the foundation of the world,"† by which the Saviour was appointed to His work of redemption. Thus "a Corner-stone" was provided for the future church before the world itself was founded.

When this "Corner-stone" was actually laid in Zion, the men who professed to be master builders in Israel rejected with contempt the "elect" of the Father. Strange that God should permit His eternally ordained One to be set aside even for a moment by His blind creatures. Strange too, it was, that these despisers of the "Corner-stone" should use the very name which indicated the heavenly mission of Christ : "If He be the *chosen* ‡ of God," was the scornful supposition by which they ignorantly came close to a truth.

It was foretold that the foundation to be laid in Zion should be "a tried stone ;" § and Christ, as the support of His people, has been proved in every age, in every land, and under all circumstances, and has never for one moment failed the trusting heart.

* 1 Peter ii. 6.   † Matt. xxi. 42.   ‡ ἐκλεκτος, Luke xxiii. 35.
§ Isaiah xxviii. 16.

His disciples may have been disciplined in dungeons,
by exile, or by a martyr's death, and men have
perhaps inquired, Where is " their help and their
shield ?"*   But as the world sees not its present
God, so it notes not the unfailing support given to
all who build on this "tried Corner-stone." The
united experience of all believers might be expressed in the well-known words of the ancient
martyr Polycarp, the friend of St. John. The old
man could have saved his body from the flames by
denying Christ, but he had " tried " the Saviour
too long to doubt His faithfulness, and replied,
" Eighty-six years have I served Him, and He has
always borne with me lovingly."†   A simple and
yet a grand confession in the face of a terrible
death.

The prophet calls this "Corner-stone" *precious;* ‡
and the apostle who had so signally tried the
patience and love of his Lord uses the same epithet,
not only to express his own feelings, but those of
all believers. §   The word clearly implies that a
Christian prefers Christ and His Gospel to honour,
power, riches, and to all which the world counts
glorious. Who among us feels that he falls short
of this ?   Let such a one weigh well the words,
" To you who believe He is precious." If one thing
be preferred to Christ, then is He so far rejected.

---

* Psalm cxv. 9.

† See the letter of the Church at Smyrna to the Church of Phila-
delphia, in Wake's Epistles of the Apostolic Fathers.

‡ Isaiah xxviii. 16.   § 1 Peter ii. 4 and 7.

Isaiah concludes his full description of "The Corner-stone" by adding the comprehensive words, "a sure foundation," thus guiding our thoughts to one great requirement of the soul, *certainty*. How can this be gained by a being who knows not what may happen the next minute? The Gospel shows the way to every Christian. It points out Christ as the only foundation on which a man should build;* it declares "that all things work together for good to them that love God;"† and then comes in the duty of humbly "casting all your care upon" the heavenly Father. ‡ This is Christianity; and surely this belief and this practice must bring to the heart that "perfect peace"§ which arises from staying the mind on "a sure foundation."

So completely is this "Corner-stone" fitted to bear up the soul in all her works for this life and the next, that it is called "a living stone." ‖ Build here, and remain in calm and holy security through all the changes of time—through all the ages of eternity. The foundation is for life; no source of decay is in it; no cause of change lies beneath or around; it cannot grow old, and bears the stamp of immortality.

Strange that this wonderful "Corner-stone" should ever be a "stone of stumbling"¶ upon which men, instead of building for eternity, fall, and are utterly broken. Perhaps this life affords no spectacle so sad as that of a soul destroying

* 1 Cor. iii. 11—15. ‡ 1 Peter v. 7. ‖ 1 Peter ii. 4.
† Rom. viii. 28. § Isa. xxvi. 3. ¶ 1 Peter ii. 8.

itself on the very rock of salvation. Yet this may
often be seen in our age by those who observe the
peculiar rashness and unreasonable self-reliance of
a certain class of minds.

The believer in Christ, who has built on a sure
and everlasting foundation, on which he now enjoys
perfect security, and where his house shall stand
safely when the earth and heavens are shaken, will,
with a grateful heart, rejoice in the support and
oneness procured for the household of faith by the
chosen, tried, precious, and living Chief Corner-
stone.

THE HEAD OF THE CHURCH.

Ephes. v. 23.   Colos. i. 18 ; ii. 19.

The Church of Christ is connected with earth and
heaven.   Her life begins in this world, but is continued and developed in the " many mansions " of
the Father's house.   No merely human head can
therefore ever be fully suited to such a spiritual
family.   The body is to have a place in the heavens;
the head must also be heavenly.   Cæsar shall have
all the honour due to Cæsar; but spiritual worship,
and the undying loyalty of the renewed heart, are
given to Jesus as " the Head of the Church."

What emphatic terms, what suggestive epithets,
was the Apostle led to employ, in order to bring

before us the close and mysterious relationship of
our Lord to His people. Had some uninspired
writer represented the Everlasting Word, " the
Lord of Hosts," under the familiar though expressive title of "Husband," or "Bridegroom,"* we
should have deemed it a great irreverence. But the
Apostle compares the relationship of the Church to
Christ as "Head," with that of a wife to her husband.
The tenderest of human associations is therefore
selected to illustrate the nature of Christ's headship.

This title reminds us of the peculiar submission
which the Church renders to her Lord ; a submission
of love and not of dread ; a submission of heart and
not of mere external reverence. The solemn majesty
which surrounds the Eternal Son as the depositary
of mediatorial power, and as the Judge of the living
and the dead, can be contemplated without terror,
when we remember that He, as "Head," rules
believers with a protecting love, similar to that
which influences a husband's heart. Infinite tenderness, unspeakable watchfulness, patience inex-
haustible, and a pity far above our conceptions, are
suggested to us by this consoling and beautiful
representation of the Lord as "the Head." The
title also suggests a remarkable contrast. The
husband ceases to be the head of the wife when
death dissolves the marriage, but no such severance
can ever happen between the divine "Head" and
His Church. Death has never yet broken that
mystical marriage bond ; the grave itself is but the

* Compare Isaiah liv. 5. with Ephes. v. 23, John iii. 29 and Rev. xxi. 2.

passage through which "the bride" approaches "the King in His beauty."* The Church never really dies, and the ever-living Redeemer will be her everlasting Head.

Death is indeed a great divider, separating the soul from her time-worn tenement, and then dissolving the house of the spirit into the dust of earth. But this apparently irresistible power cannot sunder the Church from her Head.

The Apostle uses another image to set before us the mystery of Christ's headship. Having represented the Church as a wife, and the Saviour as a husband, he varies the illustration, by comparing the whole family of believing souls to "a body," and the Lord to "the Head."† This representation sets the Lord before us as the source of all energy, the centre from which proceeds every healthy impulse. The Church, viewed in herself and apart from "the Head," is no treasury of grace, no depositary of world healing remedies. When we speak of flourishing churches, or living churches, we simply mean that Christ is living in them. When we mourn over declining churches, we are lamenting the interruption of communication with "the Head." As surely as the vessels and nerves of the natural body convey energy from the head to every part, so does the whole system of spiritual means and agencies, instituted by our Lord, communicate the richness of His grace to every Christian heart. But, as in the body, the vital energy does not reside in

* Isaiah xxxiii. 17.   † Colos. i. 18; Ephes. iv. 15, 16.

the conveying vessels, only passing through them, so spiritual power is not necessarily found in mere ordinances. Pastors, teachers, divine worship, and sacraments, are but channels through which heavenly strength is freely given to each believer. To forget this is to exalt the feeble agent, and to dishonour the great Head. The misguided heart may turn the simple means of grace into idols; looking to them only, rather than to Him from whom the whole body receives its life. This is no imaginary danger; the trust in means only, has been a delusion and a snare to many a soul.

As the Church has but one supreme "Head," her perfect oneness is thus secured. Her life flows from One, her course is guided by One, her lessons are given by One, her work allotted by One, her discipline appointed by One, her warfare directed by One, her triumph prepared by One, and her eternal weight of glory purchased by One. From this unity of divine operation it will surely come to pass, that all the members of Christ's mystical body shall in every sense "be one."* Even now, men often misjudge the nature, and exaggerate the extent of the divisions among true Christians. Differences are not always schisms, and hearts may be united though judgments diverge. But when the appointed "times of refreshing" shall come, we are sure that the Saviour's most comprehensive prayer will be answered: "all shall be one."

The doctrine of Church unity has indeed been

* John xvii. 21.

abused, and fearfully misunderstood, but the mis-
interpretations of men must not be allowed to hide
the beautiful unity which belongs to the household
of God.*   Let us labour to realize this oneness ; to
see and feel that all Christians form one body in
hallowing union with Christ, the Head. From this
conviction will spring more power, energy, life, and
victory over error, than can be produced by a thousand volumes of controversy. There have been
strivings in the Lord's camp, civil wars in Christ's
kingdom, because one member insisted upon being
called the whole body. Wider hearts, more hallowed
aims, a distinct recognition of the whole Church as
one body, and a full acknowledgment of the Saviour
as the " Head," will prove effectual remedies for
many an evil. A united Christendom might prove
a guide to this excited and inquisitive nineteenth
century, or a rampart against many a fierce attack
on social happiness and divine truth.

In the meantime let every Christian hold firmly
to the great practical doctrine of an ever-present
Redeemer, directing all things as " the Head " of
the Church. Our true prosperity depends not on
canons, however wisely framed ; not on mere organizations, however skilfully contrived ; not on the
whole machinery of external aids and advantages,
but on the vital energies communicated to us from
our loving, directing, and ever-living " Head."

* Ephes. ii. 19.

---◆---

Titles of our Lord

AS

THE FIRST AND THE LAST.

---◆---

THE AUTHOR AND FINISHER OF OUR FAITH.
THE SAME YESTERDAY, TO-DAY, AND FOR EVER.
THE ALPHA AND OMEGA.
THE LAST ADAM.
THE JUDGE OF QUICK AND DEAD.
THE AMEN.

THE above six titles represent the Saviour as the all and in all. Faith is a rich treasure, but Christ is *The Author and Finisher.* Does the soul, amidst all her vicissitudes, seek for an unchanging helper, she finds one in Him who is *The same Yesterday,*

Q

To-day, and for Ever. As *The Alpha and Omega*
we see the fulness of the Godhead dwelling in the
Redeemer who, as *The Last Adam,* employs this
divine power to restore ruined humanity to more
than its primal honour. When the great probation
of time shall be over, the Lord will further manifest
His glory as *The Judge of the Quick and Dead,*
while as *The Amen* the Saviour will set His con-
firming seal to the finished history of earth, and
the everlasting glory of His church.

The Author and Finisher of our Faith.

Heb. xii. 2.

The word here translated author is rendered
prince in Acts iii. 15 and v. 31, and *captain* in Heb.
ii. 10; but in each case the words guide our contemplations to Jesus as the origin of all good—the
leader of all souls. This title calls us to meditate
on the ever-blessed Saviour as both the beginner
and the completer of the divine life in man.

How often does the beginning of a great work
present a most startling contrast with the end !
Bright hope attends the commencement, thick darkness marks the close. He who began the work dies
before it is accomplished, and a stranger finishes
the business. But in the progress of a soul from
the dark land of sin and bondage to the glorious

liberty of the sons of God, Jesus is both the "Author and Finisher." His awakening grace and pity first called the heart from its sinful torpor, and His ever present help secures the "abundant entrance" into the everlasting kingdom. Not one redeemed spirit will ever be found which can say, "I began the work, but the Lord completed"; nor, on the other hand, will it be said by any of the saved, "The Lord began, and I finished." Thus in the secret workings of our spiritual life Christ is all and in all—"the first and the last."

But while the word "author" reminds us that our blessed and merciful Saviour is the origin of all heavenly gifts to each of His followers, there is another and more general sense in which we may contemplate Him as "The Author of Faith." He first made clear the great doctrines of the atonement for man's sin, mediation between God and men, and the resurrection to life everlasting, which had before been dimly revealed in types and prophecies. To our Lord's teaching we must ascribe the clear knowledge of "life and immortality" which Christians now possess.* It is impossible for us to realize the perplexity in which the mind was often involved before the great Light-giver came to illuminate the world. Our present information is so full, and the rays of the "sun of righteousness" shine with so pure an effulgence, that we are apt to forget it was not always so. The mockery of the Athenians "when they heard of the resurrection,"†

* 2 Tim. i. 10.   † Acts xvii. 32.

and the vain questioning of the Sadducees,* represent to some extent the general gloom in which
mankind walked before the Lord became the
"Author" of that system of faith which now
guides us heavenward.   The hallowing doctrines,
and heart supporting promises, which are training
multitudes in many lands for the life that now is
and the life which is to come, are not to be traced
to the teaching of evangelists, apostles, or disciples.
They have only handed to us the truths given to
themselves ; they originated nothing.   To speak
of the doctrines of St. Peter, the opinions of St.
Paul, or the ideas of St. John, is to forget the com-
manding influence of the divine Teacher upon the
hearts and understandings of His followers.   What
can St. John say which Christ did not teach ?   St.
Paul did not learn from Gamaliel the mysteries of
the life to come, or the glories of the Redeemer's
mediatorial kingdom.   Christ alone is "The Author"
of the faith.   Thus looking to Jesus we are compelled to take up the language of St. Peter, and
confess with adoring gratitude, "Thou hast the
words of eternal life."†

But the Saviour is also "The Finisher" or
perfecter of faith.   He has planted the tree of life
in the soil of earth, and will not abandon the work
of His own hands.   He has committed the honour
of finishing the training of each renewed heart to
no deputies.   Shall we compare spiritual life to a
tree ?   The seed was sown by the divine "sower,"

* Matt. xxii. 24—28.   † John vi. 68.

and He alone will remove the branch of His planting, in the fit time, to the paradise of God. Do we
liken the soul's growth in grace to a building?
Jesus, like Zerubbabel of old, lays the foundation,
and His hands finish the spiritual temple.* Is the
Christian's struggle represented as a race? The
voice of Christ first called the soul to begin the
course, and He stands at the end to crown with
never fading garlands those whom His aid has
made triumphant. Or, lastly, is the life of each
follower of the Lord aptly described as a fight?
The Saviour, who first summons each to march
beneath His banner, provides not only armour, but
secures victory.† Thus, from whatever side we
contemplate the work of Christ in us and for us,
we shall see Him both as " The Author and Finisher
of our Faith."

Will He so finish His work as to make us *perfect?*
The whole body of the faithful shall be presented
"a glorious church, not having spot or wrinkle ";‡
and even now the church militant is described as
having "come unto "—"the spirits of just men
made perfect." How long the interval seems
which lies between the first feeble accent of repentance—the first effort of faith, and the completion of salvation in the unclouded glory of the
heavenly home! That such a beginning should
expand into the joys of the everlasting kingdom,
may seem nothing less than a miracle of grace.
And such it is; for it possesses one mark of the

---

* Zech. iv. 9.   † 1 Cor. xv. 57.   ‡ Eph. v. 27.

miraculous, a *supernatural* character. Such a result
cannot be ascribed to the natural or acquired
energies of the human heart, these being disposed
to run in earthly channels. Man's intellect has
accomplished great things; he can pierce the Alps
or climb the Andes; but he never did, he never
will, make a road to heaven. One only accomplishes
such a work—" The Finisher of our Faith."

As the Redeemer will make the faith of His
chosen ones perfect, so He will demonstrate to the
world that the Gospel doctrines are fitted to form a
perfect social system. As yet the nations " rage
together," each doing battle for its own scheme,
with little reference to Him who shall, at the
appointed time, reduce the earth into His possession.* The wearied peoples shall yet admit the
Gospel to be " the perfection of beauty," and then
the Lord will appear as " the perfecter " of the
faith.

In holy thankfulness adore him as " The Author,"
with hallowing hope wait for Him as " The Finisher
of our Faith." Is He to you the former? doubt
not, He will surely be the latter. Has He begun
the work of heaven? then trust Him to guide you
through all the changes of time, and hold fast to
" The Finisher " of your faith.

* Psalm ii. 8.

THE SAME YESTERDAY, TO-DAY, AND FOR EVER.

Heb. xiii. 8.

All things near, and all things distant, are under
one great law of change.   From the thickly falling
leaves of autumn men have, in all ages, drawn
images to illustrate the passing away of man's
works, and the prophet uses the fading leaf to teach
the same lesson.* Even the stars of heaven are
not above the law; astronomy tells of movements
and disappearances in those sublime elevations,
which are but counterparts of terrestrial mutations.

How mysterious, how numerous are the changes
which have marked the histories of nations.   Once
mighty peoples have almost perished, their names
reminding us of many a lost chapter torn from the
records of time.   Is there nothing unchangeable,
then, on which man may build a few hopes for
eternity ?   Earth can offer nothing permanent; she
mourns, in vain, over her shattered hopes, ruined
systems, and perplexed philosophies.   But the heart
may, nevertheless, find a rest, which never has been
disturbed by the shocks of time, which cannot be
affected even by the dissolution of a world.   As the
dove found no rest on the troubled waters, so man
shall never procure repose amid the ceaseless agita-
tions of earth ; but as the dove had a safe home in

* Isa. lxiv. 6.

the ark, when all around was desolation, so the soul
may find a sure refuge in Him, who is "the same
yesterday, to-day, and for ever."

The ark was, indeed, but an imperfect symbol of
His unchangeableness; for every plank and beam of
the surprising structure has long since perished on
remote Asiatic mountains. In vain the fond traditions of Armenia assure us that Noah's vessel yet
exists, turned into stone. But Christ, the true Ark
of Salvation, remains without a change, through
times of judgment and ages of mercy. Was He
compassionate to the mourning sisters of Lazarus,
and the bereaved widow of Nain; patient with prejudiced disciples and cavilling Sadducees; gentle
before the mocking Herod; forgiving to the deriders
at Calvary, and even then mindful of the sorrowing
Mary? All this our ever-blessed Lord was "yesterday," and all this He is "to-day." The marvellous
sufferings endured on the Cross have changed the
spiritual history of mankind, but Jesus is still the
same. By His glorious ascension He became
invisible to the eyes of His disciples; no doubting
Thomas can strengthen faith by a touch, no worshipping Mary can gaze upon Him,* but all His
ancient love remains unchanging and unchangeable.
We must, however, remember, that the gracious purposes of the Saviour did not originate "yesterday,"
but are to be traced back to a period "before the
foundation of the world.† Suffering and death are
ancient, but the love of Christ is more ancient.

* John xx. 16. † 1 Peter i. 20.

Before sin had stained the earth, before the first cry of sorrow rose from man, the Lord of glory had arranged the wondrous plan of redemption. The almost total rebellion of the human race, the spread of idolatry, the rejection of the true God by nearly every nation, and the desolating violence of a long series of ages, made no change in the Redeemer's love and pity He carried out His eternal purpose by dwelling amongst men, tasting the bitterness of death, descending into the gloom of the grave, and rising triumphantly with the keys of hell and of death.

Eighteen centuries have passed, and the loving Lord is the same " to-day," as when He washed the feet of the wondering disciples, and with a look brought Peter to repentance.* He has beheld large sections of the visible Church forgetting Him in creature worship, and hiding His perfect sacrifice by pompous rites. But to every trusting heart, looking to Him for life and light, He says " to-day," as to Simon in old times, " blessed art thou."†

We are continually changing, and are too apt to suppose that He changes also. The two disciples, discoursing on the road about their altered prospects and ruined hopes, knew not their Master, even though He was talking with them, unchanged in wisdom and in love.‡ Christians now have their special seasons of hope, faith, and love, when they feel more trust in Christ than at other times. Yet their Lord is ever " the same," always trustworthy,

* Luke xxii. 61.   † Matt. xvi. 17.   ‡ Luke xxiv. 13—35.

always accessible, always pitiful and of great kindness. Say not, rashly, that He withholds His
presence; when the fact is, that the unstable disciple
has wandered. But it is easy for the careless and
inconstant servant to blame the unchangeable
Master.

As the Saviour is "the same" at all times, and in
all ages, so His Gospel system speaks alike in all
periods of the world's history. It has not one
message for a rude, and another for a civilized age;
not one statement for the unreasoning multitude,
and another for the critical few. As the sun sheds
the same light on the untaught child, and on the
wisest of mankind, so the same healing beams come
from the Sun of Righteousness to men of every degree.
Earthly lights may, and must, change with each
passing gust of human opinion, but no storm of
earth can affect the sun. What the Gospel message
was to men of the first century, that it will be to
men of the last.' The increase of learning, the
improvement of criticism, and the development of
science, may enable the Church to proclaim with
more power, and to defend with more wisdom, the
word of reconciliation; but the words of life, like the
Lord of Life, are ever "the same." All earnest,
truthful, and loving Christian hearts may therefore
receive, from the lessons of the past and the experience of the present, fresh motives for a humble, but
decisive trust in His guidance, who is "the same
yesterday, to-day, and for ever."

THE ALPHA AND OMEGA.

Rev. i. 8, 11; xxi. 6; xxii. 13.

The alphabet of a language contains all the signs
by which the whole literature and science of the
nation are expressed. The wisest of the ancient
Greeks, a Homer, a Plato, or a Thucydides, was
compelled to hand down to distant ages all his
eloquence and knowledge in the twenty-four letters
from Alpha to Omega. It was therefore natural
that completeness or perfection should be expressed
by saying, "It is the Alpha and Omega." Thus
the Lord Jesus Christ declares to us in this short,
but most expressive formula, His divine glory and
eternal attributes.

These words direct our contemplations to that
mysterious period, when the Eternal Godhead was
the only being; when there was no universe, no
angel, no spirit. They remind us of the first miracle
wrought in the universe—the Creation; when the
Lord manifested Himself as "the Alpha"—the
beginning.

So grand a title suggests ideas too vast, too
remote from our thoughts for a full comprehension;
but it may well lead us to meditate with a holy awe,
and yet with a quiet confidence, on the glory of the
Redeemer.

The Lord is the "Alpha and Omega"; therefore

in Him the whole circle of Revelation is complete.
He was revealed in the beginning of Genesis,* and
His second coming is proclaimed at the close of that
wondrous vision which John saw in Patmos.† All
doctrine centres in Him ; not one heavenly intimation
can be found in the whole sacred record, which
does not point directly, or by implication, to the
Saviour of the World.   All the morality of the Bible
is based upon Christ, the acceptability of our works
depending upon His mediation.   He is the cause of
the whole spiritual and material system, "for by Him
were all things created that are in heaven and that
are in earth."‡   He thus appears as the mysterious
and adorable " Alpha," whose creative energies are
as yet but dimly seen in their far-off manifestations.
In the light of heaven we may hope to behold the
nearer brightness of His works.   The Saviour is also
"the Omega," it having been the Father's pleasure
that "for Him" the whole universe should exist.§
This is amazing ; reason gives up all attempts to
deal with so divine and vast a plan ; we receive the
revelation with adoring joy, and unite with the
heavenly host in the hymn of triumph, "Worthy is
the Lamb that was slain."‖

The early Christians, who were trained by a per-
secuting world to a constant looking unto Jesus, so
fully realized the appropriateness and comprehensiveness of this title of the Lord, that these two
letters, the Alpha and Omega, were sometimes

---

* Genesis iii. 15.   † Rev. xxii. 20.   ‡ Col. i. 16.
§ Col. i. 16.   ‖ Rev. v. 12.

sculptured on their tombs. Some of these interesting inscriptions have been rescued from their ancient sites in the catacombs of Rome. There in the old days of evangelical purity the faithful dead were buried in the deep gloom of those subterranean vaults, where the fierce heathen could not discover their quiet resting-places.* Faith can well maintain the conflict of time, while keeping near to Him who is the beginning of all life and power; and in holy resignation she can finish her earthly work, relying on the Saviour, for whom as "the Omega" all things were formed.

This title was declared by Christ Himself, who alone knows perfectly His own infinite perfections. The announcement was not made during His sojourn on earth; so grand a communication being reserved until He had taken possession of the mediatorial throne. It is nearly the last of those magnificent titles by which the exalted Lord was pleased to reveal His glory to those persecuted followers, from whom the brightness of His presence was for awhile hidden. The last book of the Scriptures fitly contains such a title. After the voluntary humiliation of Messiah, after the amazing trials of His earthly life had been suffered; after the triumph over the grave had been witnessed, and the heavens had received Him; then there was indeed a peculiar fitness in proclaiming the mighty Lord to mankind as the " Alpha and Omega."

* Some of these inscriptions are now preserved in the Vatican.

It was a special memorial day, " the Lord's day,"*
when this title was first announced, and the Apostle
probably received the revelation in his gloomy prison
in the depths of the Patmos mines. In what lonely,
what lowly places, does the mighty God sometimes
make Himself known. To Jacob in the dark night
on a lonely waste ;† to Moses in the solitudes of
Horeb ;‡ to the faithful Jews in the midst of the
fire ;§ and to the beloved disciple in a subterraneous
dungeon. He who opened the future history of time
to the eyes of John, could, in a moment, have delivered him from a Roman prison. But it was His
pleasure to visit the disciple in the mine. Never
had a dark prison house received before such a flood
of heavenly light. That was, probably, the brightest
Lord's day in the Apostle's long life. Was not the
aged John then as truly the beloved disciple, as
when at the Paschal supper he leaned on the breast
of Jesus ?‖

If we have received the Lord Jesus as the "Alpha
and Omega" of our souls, let us not judge Him by
feeble sense, or weak reason, but confide in His
abiding faithfulness. This title proclaims His uncreated and eternal divinity, and has surely been
declared to strengthen our faith in Him, who being
the fulness of the Godhead, will withhold no good
thing from the obedient and trusting disciples.

---

* Rev. i. 10.   † Gen. xxxii. 24-30.   ‡ Exod. iii. 1—4.
§ Dan. iii. 25.   ‖ John xiii. 23.

THE LAST ADAM.

1 Cor. xv. 45.

We always listen with an eager, and certainly
with an allowable curiosity, to all particulars respecting the primitive condition of mankind. We speculate
on the moral and intellectual state of Adam; the
nature of his occupations, the time of his abode in
Eden, the position of that first home of man, and
especially the early introduction of sin and sorrow
into the newly-formed earth. But amidst these
subjects of contemplation, there arises on the field
of view, that one dark and portentous event, which
rivets the mournful gaze of the wisest men. We
see Adam, the head of the new race, changed from
the first human worshipper of God into the first
human rebel against his Creator. We see the
terrestrial paradise turned into a desert, and the
pure and bright angels themselves engaged in
driving man from his beautiful primeval home.*
The traditions of many lands have borne the mournful story down from age to age, and it forms the
first sorrowful narrative in the sacred record.

Men speculate still on the origin of evil; but soon
the wisest find how utterly unable they are to get
beyond the history given in Genesis. As sin has
entered the world, and death is present, the im-

* Gen. iii. 24.

portant question is, not how did they originate, but
how can they be remedied ?   At the first glance
hope dies.   How is it possible to escape from sin
and death ?   Nature is silent.   Man may torture
himself in vain, like the priests of Baal, in the
attempt to get a reply, but there is not "any to
answer."

The first Adam could not rebuild the ruined house
of man; the nine hundred and thirty years of his
life shewed him the fatal energy of sin.   Death first
revealed its awful power to the first man, in the
murdered body of his son, and the sullen rage of
Cain was the forerunner of long ages of malice and
war.   The first head of the human family descended
to the grave, having found no antidote to the poison
which he had given to his children.

At this critical point the Saviour offers Himself
to our view as the "Last," or Second Adam, one
commissioned to reverse, in the case of all who
accept Him, the consequences flowing from the sin
of the first.

As Adam became the head of a mortal race, all
having died in him, so Christ has become the head
of an immortal family, for in Him "shall all be
made alive."*   The remedy shall be as wide as the
calamity.   "All" enter the grave, but "all" shall
rise again.   If the first man brought death upon
"the many,"† Christ died for "the whole world";‡
if the first Adam became the subject of death, the
"Last Adam" "hath abolished death."§   Is not

* Cor. xv. 22.   † Rom. v. 15.   ‡ 1 John ii. 2.   § 2 Tim. i. 10.

the reversal complete ? In this sense, as the head
of a new and immortal race, the eternal Son may be
fitly called " the everlasting Father,"* for He is the
giver of that "eternal life,"† which is the heritage
of His chosen ones.

The first Adam was made "a living soul,"‡ and
forfeited even that gift of life ; but the second became " a quickening spirit," not only having eternal
life in Himself, but bestowing it upon a multitude
which no man can number.

The first Adam was made a king, under God, of
the world, being solemnly invested with dominion
" over every living thing.§ This royalty was wholly
lost, and the very earth offered its late sovereign
" thorns and thistles."‖ But Christ, as the " Last
Adam," restores to all who receive Him, a regal
dignity, making them "kings" unto God.¶ The
full extent and honour of this heavenly kingship
will not be known, until we shall be admitted into
the palace of the eternal King. But we may be
sure that the gift of Christ will far transcend in
glory all the honours lost by the fall. The Apostle,
when contrasting the destructive work of the first
with the restorative work of the second Adam, does
not for a moment regard the Redeemer as merely
replacing regenerate men in the state from which
Adam fell.** He exhibits the Saviour as providing
a remedy far more extensive than the disease.

* Isaiah ix. 6.   ‡ 1 Cor. xv. 45.   ‖ Gen. iii. 18.
† John xvii. 2.   § Gen. i. 28.   ¶ Rev. i. 6.
** See the remarkable contrast, Rom. v. 15—19.

R

The first Adam was, immediately after his sin,
clothed by the God against whom he had trans-
gressed; the "coats of skins" being, probably,
obtained from the victims then first typically offered.
The Second Adam provides the "white raiment"*
of His perfect righteousness, for all who receive His
"counsel," and accept the invitation to the marriage
supper of the Lamb. Adam's clothing, though given
by his Creator, must have become old, but the
"garments of salvation," and "the robe of righteousness,"† though "beautiful"‡ exceedingly, shall
be "everlasting."§

The first Adam was made "in the image of God;"
soon the divine likeness was lost, and the portrait
of humanity, as drawn by the hand of an Apostle,‖
shews how far man had gone from original righteousness. The "Last Adam" will wholly restore
the divine image in all who receive Him as their
Prince and Saviour. Even now He gives them
"power to become the sons of God;"¶ they are all
"to be conformed to the image" of the Son,** and
He is "the image of the invisible God." We are
unable fully to imagine the bliss of that state, when
the whole purified Church shall be "without spot or
blemish," being transformed by the grace of the
regenerating spirit, and preserved from all future
fall by the power of the ever present Saviour. "Ye
shall be as Gods,"†† were the words of the tempting

* Rev. iii. 18 & xix. 8.   § Dan. ix. 24.   ** Rom. viii. 29.
† Isaiah lxi. 10.   ‖ See Rom. i.   †† Gen. iii. 5.
‡ Isaiah lii. 1.   ¶ John i. 12.

spirit in Eden ; the lying promise of the fiend has become expressive of a high and glorious truth ; fallen men, when renewed, do become " like " unto God.*

The first Adam was " earthy," being from the earth, and returning thither. The burial place of the first man is unknown, but we are sure that the sentence, " unto dust shalt thou return," was fully executed. The " Last Adam " is the " Lord from heaven,"† and thither He has taken the body of His glory, which no tomb could retain. The sons of the earthy Adam followed in long succession, and are following still, their ancestor to the grave. He has no power to recover one of his earth-imprisoned children. To the " Last Adam " this mighty work pertains. Not only will He raise all the dead, and thus confer immortality on the human body,‡ but will translate into the everlasting mansions the raised bodies of all believers.

The first Adam soon lost his paradise, not remaining in it long enough for one of his children to behold its beauties. Strange fables have in vain tried to supply information which the Spirit of Revelation has seen fit to withhold. One poet§ represents the first man as spending six hours only in Paradise. It is enough for us to know that he soon lost his blissful home ; and still more important to remember, that the " Last Adam " has opened the gates of heaven to all believers. No bright

* 1 John iii. 2.   † 1 Cor. xv. 47.   ‡ 1 Cor. xv. 42.
§ Dante. Paradise xxvi. 142.

cherubim are now stationed to keep man from the heavenly paradise, the holy angels being ever ready to be "ministering spirits" to the heirs of salvation.*

The restoration thus secured by the Second Adam is complete for all who confide in Him as their Mediator. His work is perfect; but its perfection is far beyond our present powers to apprehend. We can receive from our divine Head more than Adam lost. We cannot expect too much. Righteousness, life, a heavenly kingdom, and the joys of an eternal paradise, are all offered by Christ, the "Last Adam."

THE JUDGE OF QUICK AND DEAD.

Acts x. 42.

The idea of a future Judgment, kept under some restraint even the more wicked among the pagans of old times. Over the more thoughtful, the gloomy shadows of the judgment hall fell with a chilling influence. As death drew near, the trembling mortal multiplied his sacrifices, and sought, by many a costly rite, the favour of the unseen Judge.

The Gospel also reveals to us the certainty of a judgment to come, and names the Judge of the

* Heb. i. 14.

living and the dead. In Christ are united the
apparently opposite offices of Mediator and Judge.
How often do we find that the fulness of the
Redeemer's work can be expressed by contrasts
only. Thus He is represented as a Lion and a
Lamb; as Son of man, and Son of God; the Alpha
and yet the Omega; the Advocate, and also the
Judge. So various are the offices involved in the
mediation of the Saviour, so many sided are its
aspects, that it is only by seeming opposites the
whole can be pourtrayed.

Our Propitiation is to be our Judge. What
startling contrasts does this suggest. Could Pilate
have seen, but for a moment, that the accused and
silent Jesus would one day be on the judgment
throne, with what horror would he have rushed from
his seat. The Jewish council sentenced Him, before
whom each elder of Judæa would hereafter stand,
while a world looked on in amazement. The Lord
allowed the judicial charge to be written over His
hallowed head on the Cross, He having before that
hour been "ordained of God to be Judge of quick
and dead."

We have here another instance of the hiding of
His glory, in which part of the Lord's voluntary
humiliation consisted. The Judge of the World
walked among men, sat at their feasts, mingled in
their sorrows, and listened to their insults, but they
knew not that the Father had then "committed all
judgment unto the Son."*

* John v. 22.

The precise manner of the great Judgment, the period which such a stupendous event may occupy, or the age of the world in which "the Judge" will manifest Himself, are indeed concealed. But that such a period is approaching, a day in which the once crucified Jesus will judge the world, is among the sure verities of God.

As the judgment will stand alone in man's history an event without a parallel—a climax to the works of time; so the Judge unites in Himself most marvellous characteristics. How easy for Him to judge all men who has seen and has intimately known the whole life, inner and outer, of every human being! From the first thought in Adam's heart, to the last good or evil deed on the earth, all will be open unto "Him with whom we have to do."*

The Judge of the world is also the Lawgiver of the world; and all the impenitent violators of the heavenly ordinances, all obstinate resisters of divine influence, all despisers of the silent and oft-repeated admonitions of the great heart-teacher, will see on the throne the utterer of these calls to repentance and faith. The supremacy of the Judge, and the kingly character He sustains, will necessarily stamp *finality* on the proceedings of the judgment day. As there can be no error, no want of knowledge in the Judge, there can never be any rectification of His decision. But if final, it must be everlasting; and this is the solemn character ascribed to this

* Heb. iv. 13.

wonderful day in all the descriptions vouchsafed to us. There will be but one judgment; thus a peculiar *oneness* is stamped on man's history. One birth introduces him to one state of probation and grace; one Saviour opens the gate to one heaven; and one death is introductory to one judgment.

Among the amazing phenomena of that day must be placed the fact that the Judge will be visible. All the representations given of this coming day of wonders compel us to expect a sensible manifestation of Christ as "The Judge of Quick and Dead." We may therefore venture, without presumption, on the attempt to realize, by silent, deep, and prayerful thought, a little of this most awful, most grand manifestation. We shall then see the glorified body of our ever-blessed Saviour;* the attending of the angelic host;† strange appearances in the heavens;‡ mighty changes in the whole system of nature;§ the raised dead of all ages and nations, separated by no distinctions, except that of saved and lost;‖ the emotions of all generations, the events of all time concentrated into a day; and the approaching everlasting separation of the whole human family into two communities only¶; all this must make a day, the glory or the "terrors" of which alike transcend our power fully to realize. We shall each one see it all; many a wondrous event may shake the earth in which we shall have no share,

---

* Acts i. 11, and 1 John iii. 2. † Matt. xxv. 31. ‡ Matt. xxiv. 30.
§ 2 Pet. iii. 10. ‖ Matt. xxv. 32. ¶ Matt. xxv. 46.

but at the judgment we shall all certainly be present.

Some can even now contemplate this great day, and without one trembling, hesitating feeling, say, "Even so, come, Lord Jesus."* These will arise from the dust of the earth, prepared for judgment as for a heavenly jubilee, and ready to utter their holy joy in the ancient strain of the church in olden times, "This is our God, we have waited for Him."†

Let us not forget that our Lord is judging, approving, or condemning us now. In this sense He is an ever-present, ever-acting Judge. Each hour of life produces a work of some kind for or against the Saviour. He has shown how we may see with joy the throne of judgment, and hear with delight the final decision. Is not the Judge our propitiation and mediator? Is He not also the way, the truth, and the life? Then to hail Him with delight as our Judge, we must receive Him in those characters. If now His cross be our refuge, His throne of judgment will become our joy for ever.

The Amen.

Rev. iii. 14.

The word "Amen," derived from the Hebrew noun "*aumēn*," signifying truth, is used by Christians,

* Rev. xxii 20.　　† Isaiah xxv. 9.

Jews, and even Mahommedans in their worship.
The term had become to the religious Jews so expressive of divine verity, that no mistake could arise
when our Lord applied this particular title to Himself. All would feel that he claimed one of these
divine attributes, for when the prophet describes
Jehovah as "the God of truth,"* *Amen* (aumēn) is
used in the original by the inspired writer. The
varied use of the word in the New Testament will
suggest to all thoughtful believers many profitable
themes for holy meditation.

Sometimes the Saviour employed this emphatic
term to prepare the mind of a listener for the re-
ception of some vital truth. When about to enforce
upon the truth-seeking, yet timid Nicodemus, the
necessity of a divine regeneration for the human
soul, the Great Teacher prefaced His holy lesson by
the repetition of the words, "Amen, Amen."† Our
mediator is not only the author of truth, but the
preparer of the way by which the saving message
enters the hearts of men, and penetrates into the
seats of pagan darkness. The "Amen" sends forth
the awakening voice either of Providence or of His
Holy Spirit, and the people are thus made willing
in the day of His power.

"Amen," is a term of confirmation by which the
seal is put to a writing, or a solemn approval given
to a spoken message. Each of the gospels, and

---

* Isaiah lxv. 16, *i.e.*, "The God of Truth,"—"The God of Amen."

† John iii. v. The reader perhaps should be reminded that the
"verily" of the English version is often the translation of amen.

every epistle, excepting James and the third of
John, close with this expressive word, which is also
the last in the Bible. Thus the "lively oracles"
end with a word which speaks of truth settled upon
a sure foundation, and sealed with the signet of the
King of heaven. How often, and in what diversified methods, has the Lord stamped His divine
approval on the Gospel message, even though
uttered by the weakest of His servants. His salvation has been offered to multitudes of the weary and
heavy laden, who have heard in the depth of their
spirits the voice of the "Amen" speaking His
blessed confirmation to their hearts. And the
divine seal of His approbation has never been
broken, for the "Amen" has a permanence which
is of heaven.

The whole Gospel system might be characterized
as "Amen," inasmuch as it bears the mark of a
divine stamp upon its history, and has duration
marked on every part. To stand for a day is no
proof of a well-built house; to triumph for centuries
amid the evil or the ignorant is no mark of a true
religion. But to abide through all ages, to be
suited to every land, adapted to each variety of
human life and all ages of man's history, this is
truly the seal of God set upon the doctrines and
precepts of the Gospel. Christianity has never
changed to suit any people, or to accommodate
itself to any state of society, but by its divine adaptation to man's need has transformed the social
aspect of many nations, and introduced the prin-

ciples of a heavenly life into a multitude of souls.
The thoughtful, the wise-hearted, the lovers of God,
and the friends of men, listen to the divine teachings of the Lord, and all respond with a solemn
"Amen." Surely none but the desperate, the
despisers of men, or the neglecters of God, would
say of the Gospel, "Let it perish." If a few such
exist, their foolish cry would be drowned by the
loud and heartfelt "Amen" of multitudes.

By this title the Saviour may have intended to
teach us how perfectly we may rely upon Him for
all things. "All the promises of God in Him"
are Amen,* and shall therefore be accomplished.
Look carefully at the golden roll of the promises;
see by faith those which are spoken to you as an
individual Christian, and those which are spoken to
the whole united church of God. All are sure, for
the "Amen" has uttered them. His holy name is
affixed to each. Much is yet to be done in you,
much is yet to be done for you; the promises contain your future history, unless indeed by repeated
resistance of the Holy Spirit you are punished by a
loss of privileges, and permitted to become spirit-
ually blind and hard of hearing.

The Jewish rabbins have in certain ages of
superstition taught that the loud utterance of the
word "Amen" would open the gates of paradise.
What they vainly hoped from the literal we may
justly seek from the spiritual "Amen." From
heaven our glorious Lord proclaimed this His title,

* 2 Cor. i. 20.

that by daily, stedfast, humble, and obedient trust
in Him, we should at "the end of days" meet Him
in perfect peace.   On earth we shall never know
the full force of this name of our Saviour; but
when the warfare shall be accomplished, and faith
has laid down Her shield at His feet, then the pardoned and emancipated spirit will adore in the pure
home of heaven her eternal Amen.

London:—William Macintosh, 24, Paternoster Row.

www.ingramcontent.com/pod-product-compliance
Lightning Source LLC
Chambersburg PA
CBHW031425020726
47499CB00005B/1604